I0716822

Lilith

RETRIBUTION KINGS BOOK 4

ELLA MILES

Retribution Kings Series

Lennox (Book 1)
Rialta (Book 2)

Hayes (Book 3)
Lilith (Book 4)

Gage (Book 5)
Nova (Book 6)

The Retribution Kings Series is a spinoff of the Retribution Games Series. If you want to read Beckett and River's story, start with Mistaken Hero

CHAPTER 1

Hayes

I OPEN the hotel room door, unsure of what I'm about to find. Based on Lilith's threats against me, I shouldn't be here. I should be talking to Titus or running before he decides to give Lilith what she wants and kill me. But this is too important. It can't wait.

The door falls closed behind me as I walk quickly into the room, a determined set to my steps. I have a mission to do, and I can't fail. This has to work.

There is no reason this should fail. I have a perfect record, and I've spent weeks studying Ruby and her husband, Samson. I know exactly how to play this.

Except my mind is focused on a different fiery redhead—one who promised to kill me. When I should be focused on the very naked woman in my bed.

I stop, leaning against the wall next to the bed; I fold my arms across my chest and smirk at Ruby, my eyes roaming up and down her bare body like a starving man about to devour a feast.

Ruby should be weary after seeing me with Lilith. But

she's so desperate for a man to show her affection that she's not thinking straight.

It will make my job that much easier.

Ruby is lying on the bed with her legs spread, her pussy bare, and her nipples hard under my stare.

"Hmm, whatever should I do with you," I purr, cocking my head with a mischievous smile, pretending to think of every dirty and depraved position I could fuck her in.

"Whatever you want, sir," Ruby says, running her tongue over her bottom lip and letting her hand run down the front of her chest.

Sir—there would be times when having a woman call me that would have undone me. I would have pounded into her so fast just to hear her say the word again and enjoyed pulling every indecent sound I could muster out of her.

Now, my cock barely twitches in her direction.

But I have a job to do, and no matter the cost, I'll do it.

I smile wickedly. Just as I always do.

"Turn over," I tell her as I move toward the bed.

She licks her lips in anticipation and then does as I say, turning onto her hands and knees on the bed.

I walk to the foot of the bed, getting a perfect view of her ass, ready for me.

My stomach flips, and I push down the bile that rises in my throat at what I'm about to do.

I climb up the bed behind her, my hand grabbing onto her hips roughly, stoking a groan from her body.

"Have you been a bad girl?" I ask, knowing exactly the kind of talk that will turn her on and make her putty in my hands.

My hand rubs over her ass in a slow circle while I wait for her answer.

"Yes," she barks out.

"Then you should be punished." I slap my hand over her ass hard enough that she yelps at the pain.

I rub my hand over another spot and watch as she tries to pull away before I slap her ass again.

"Uh-uh, you deserve five slaps; only then will we consider if you'd paid enough for your sins to earn being properly fucked."

She pants, and I know she's surprised by the sting of my slaps and isn't sure if she wants more. But I know the best way to get her on my side is to push her. To get her out of her head and only thinking with her pussy.

I slap her ass again. "Two."

Her body jolts at the slap. "Oh, fuck."

"Three." My hand makes contact again.

"Jesus, I can't handle more."

"You can, baby. You know you need to be punished—with my hand, then my tongue, and then you'll earn my cock."

"Yes," she moans at my words.

And then I slap her reddening ass again. "Four."

Her ass cheeks clench together, and she looks over her shoulder with tears in her eyes.

"Should I stop?" I ask.

"No," she moans.

"Five." I slap her again; the second my hand hits, I spread her legs and slide between them. I drag her ass on top of my mouth, and my tongue dives between her lips without thinking.

She gasps as I slide my tongue up her slit, finding her sensitive clit. Knowing that the sensations are going to bring her more pleasure when contrasted with the slaps I just gave her.

My tongue sweeps across her again, and the moans she

makes tell me she's close to coming on my face in a matter of seconds.

I smile cynically, increasing my speed. The faster she comes, the faster this can be over—for both of us.

I devour her hungrily, tasting her far too sweet wetness and the wrongness of the sounds she's making.

Lilith's whimpers, soft moans, and delicious scent flash through my head, but I push those thoughts away. But they invade my thoughts, even as Ruby comes hard and fast on my lips.

I squeeze my eyes shut, forcing myself to stay in the present.

Ruby collapses on my head, making it hard for me to breathe.

I chuckle beneath her, and she eventually raises her leg enough for me to roll out from underneath her.

Ruby's eyes blaze as she looks at me, panting hard. "That was—Jesus, I've never felt anything like that."

I sneer. "I know."

She laughs at my response.

I move up the bed, lying next to her. She lies her head on the pillow, staring at me with awe.

"Give me five minutes to recover from that, and then I'll be ready for you to fuck me."

My eyes darken. "Are you sure you can handle me?"

She bites her lip, seriously thinking it over like she isn't sure if she can handle me or not.

"No, but I'm going to try."

I chuckle, stroking her cheek in a loving manner. "You were friends with Iris?"

She stills under my touch. "Iris? Yes, I knew her, but I wouldn't have called her a friend. Why?"

"I've heard rumors that she's alive."

Ruby sits up suddenly, no longer allowing my touch or

looking me in the eyes.

I was right about her; she knows the truth of what happened.

"Where is Iris?" I say, gripping her bicep and turning her to face me.

Ruby grabs at the sheets, suddenly uncomfortable with being naked in front of you.

"I don't know anything about what happened to Iris."

"You do, I know you do."

She shakes her head, trembling slightly in my grasp. "That's what this was about? That's why you're here, in this bed? To get information out of me?"

"You are a smart one."

She frowns, her eyes widening in fear when she should be glaring at me in anger. Planning her revenge—that's what Lilith would be doing.

I shake that thought away.

She moves to get up, but I pull her to me. "If you are smart, then tell me everything you know about Iris, and you'll walk out of here unharmed and only think about the good time we just had together. I'll even let you ride my pierced cock for your good behavior."

She grits her teeth together in an explosion of anger. "You bastard."

I cock my head to one side.

"Are you going to rape me?"

I snort. "No, if I fucked you—you'd enjoy it too much."

And then I whistle to Gage, realizing the only way to get through to Ruby is waiting outside the door.

Gage pushes Samson, her husband, through the door.

"What the hell?" he stumbles into the room with wide eyes, glaring at us both.

I grab my gun and aim it at Ruby's head. Tears immediately start rolling down her face, and she shakes viciously next to me.

Jesus Christ, this woman is something else. Already trembling, and I've barely threatened her.

But hopefully, her tears will get Samson to talk faster.

"Tell me where Iris is, or I'll kill your wife?"

"She'd deserve it, the cheating whore!" he spits in his wife's face.

I turn my gun, firing in Samson's direction, but purposefully missing.

"I don't care about your marital problems, Samson. What I care about is you telling me where Iris is, or I'll fuck your wife in front of you and then kill you, leaving that memory the last thing you see before you die."

Samson shoots daggers in my direction.

"I'm not a patient man. Tell me where Iris is."

"You better hope he kills you. It will be faster and less painful than how I intend on killing you," Samson barks at his wife.

Ruby narrows her eyes at him. "He knows where Iris is. I'm sorry I don't. But Samson does."

"I know," I say, glaring at Samson.

Ruby looks at me, putting her arm gently on my bicep. Her tears gone.

"Fuck me. If I'm going to die, then I'd rather die after fucking a man who actually knows how to use his cock, instead of a drunk who can barely get his dick up."

I snicker. I won't be fucking her, but this is going better than I planned. She'd find my cock as limp as her husband's usually is.

Samson grinds his teeth together. "If you fucking lay another hand on her, I'll kill you."

"Tell me where Iris is. Or I'll do as I say. I'll fuck your wife just before Gage puts a bullet in your head."

"She's dead! You're too late," Samson cackles. "She died three months ago."

No.

Fuck, no.

I look to Ruby, who has tears in her eyes. "Do you believe him?"

The tear rolling down her cheek tells me yes.

She nods.

And I drive a bullet through Samson's head. Watching as he falls to the ground dead.

Gage looks at me in a way that tells me this is all my fault. And it is.

I stand from the bed.

"Deal with Ruby," I tell Gage.

He nods, but his look is disapproving.

I fucked up.

Iris is dead.

There is no way I can fix it.

But I have to try.

CHAPTER 2

Lilith

TITUS PLACES two shots of tequila on the table as he slides into the booth that Hayes was occupying a few moments earlier. After our conversation, Hayes left—most likely to follow Ruby to the hotel room. There is no doubt in my mind that he's fucking her right now.

I let him live—for now.

But right now, my rage is focused on the man in front of me.

"You knew," I say, grinding my teeth together.

Titus's lips thin, and he sighs. "If you're asking, did I know that Hayes was the one who killed your father, then yes, I did know."

I shake my head, my anger freely flowing through me.

"You made that promise knowing that I wouldn't want to kill Hayes because he tricked me into falling in love with him."

"I made that promise because it was the only way I could get you to consider my proposal."

I glare at him.

But Titus looks as relaxed as ever sitting across from me.

"Why me? Why did you choose me to be your wife?"

He stills for a moment, gathering his thoughts before he answers. "Because I need a strong woman by my side. A woman with certain skills. Skills that you possess."

I narrow my eyes. "And why do you need my skills?"

"I'll tell you as soon as we're married. After we're married, there won't be any more secrets between us."

I frown. "I don't trust you. I never will. I won't trust any man ever again." *Not after Hayes.*

"I know, but I trust you. And I have hope that someday I'll earn your trust." His eyes look at me brightly, and I can see the hope there. He really does believe what he's saying.

"You'll be waiting a long time to earn my trust."

"I know, and I'll wait however long you need. But I need you to know as much truth as I can tell you now. If you become my wife, your life won't become safer. In fact, it will be more dangerous. There will always be a target on your back. Always."

"I'm not afraid to die."

He nods as if he already knows that's how I feel.

"But it would go a long way toward me trusting you if you told me why you chose me of all people, now."

He shakes his head. "It would endanger your life, and I could offer you little protection until we're married. Only then will I tell you everything—risk everything."

I grind my teeth together, hating how this conversation is going. The only good thing about this conversation is it keeps me from thinking about Hayes. About how I hate him, love him, want to murder him, and live happily ever after with him all at the same time.

"Our agreement was I marry you, and you'll help me get revenge," I say.

"Yes," he nods.

"I don't see how you'll keep our agreement. Hayes is

your friend, or at the very least, your number two. Are you really going to help me kill him?"

Titus's jaw ticks. "Yes, I'll help you kill him if that's what you want."

"But you don't think I'll want to kill Hayes."

Titus doesn't answer.

"Why? Why would you kill Hayes? Do you think he deserves to die for killing my father?"

"No, I don't think Hayes deserves to die for killing your father. It was an order he was given by the temporary head of the Retribution Kings, and he followed it."

I raise my eyebrows at him. "See, I knew you wouldn't help me kill him."

"I will. If you want him captured, punished, killed—I'll help with whatever you want."

"Why?"

"Because you're more valuable to me than Hayes."

I swallow hard, my stomach twisting into knots at not knowing the whole truth. Not knowing why I'm so valuable. But I intend to find out.

Titus reaches into his pocket and pulls out a black box. He slides it across the table to me, not even bothering to open the box.

I stare at it—knowing it holds my future in how I answer the next question. And I'm still not sure what I want.

"Marry me, Lilith, and then I'll tell you everything."

"So romantic," I say sarcastically.

"This isn't about romance. It never will be. I don't talk about love because I doubt you'll ever fall in love with me if you can't trust me. But I hope we can align ourselves together for a common cause. Marry me and find out."

He opens the box, and a black diamond stares back at

me. It's beautiful. I've never had a piece of jewelry of any value before. I can't imagine how it'd feel to wear this.

I don't know what I want, but I do know one thing I need. And no matter how I answer, I'll figure out the rest soon enough.

"Lennox, the leader of the Corsi mafia, has my sisters. Hayes sent them to be protected by him. But I don't trust that they are safe. Help me get them back. Help me protect them. Help me keep them safe from this world."

"Done," Titus answers before I even finish speaking. "What else? I'll agree to almost anything. Even after we're married, I want you to be happy. I want us to help one another. I don't intend to force you into anything."

"No, you just tricked me and manipulated me by sending your second to make me fall in love with him."

Titus winces slightly at my words. "I'm sorry for that. I never expected a woman as strong as you to fall in love so quickly."

I frown, my eyes dropping to the shot glass that I still haven't drunk.

I lift it.

Titus lifts his to me.

I nod, and we both slam our heads back, downing the liquid in one gulp.

I take the ring from the box and slip it on the tip of my ring finger. I feel Titus staring at me with a growing smile on his face.

"And what of Hayes?" Titus asks.

"Let me worry about Hayes. Whatever I decide, you'll honor?"

Titus nods. "Whatever you want—I'll do. Now or fifty years from now. The decision will always be yours."

I push the ring all the way on. "Then arrange the wedding."

CHAPTER 3

Hayes

I STAND in front of Lennox's condo, but I can't bring myself to knock. My eyes bore into the thick wooden door as if it has all the answers.

Gage silently approaches from behind. He doesn't say anything—there is nothing to say.

Pain ripples through my body at the thought of what I'm about to do. I fucked up more than I ever have in my life. And now Lennox is going to pay for it. He's endured enough. He shouldn't have to suffer any more than he already has.

Minutes pass, though, and I don't knock. I'm sure Lennox knows I'm here. But whatever he sees on his security cameras stops him from opening the door.

"It's going to be okay," Gage says, gripping my shoulder in what is supposed to be a comforting gesture. Instead, it feels like a knife jabbing into my shoulder. I don't deserve to be reassured by a friend.

I shake his hand off my shoulder and hear his sigh. He's disappointed in me even if he's here for me now. But I know he's really here to comfort Lennox.

In one fluid motion, I lift my hand and knock rapidly on the door.

It opens immediately, and I see a wide-eyed Lennox usher us inside. "What are you doing here? Don't you know it's not safe? Vincent Corsi could have me kill you both, or Titus could order you to kill me for this betrayal."

Tears well in my eyes, and my throat suddenly runs dry. I can't form any words.

I expect Gage to step in—to save me—but he doesn't. I need to be the one to tell Lennox.

"Where is Rialta?" I ask.

"She's with Vincent."

I nod. *Good, she doesn't need to be here for this conversation.*

"Why are you here?" Lennox growls at us. He should only blame me. This isn't Gage's fault.

"We're here because I fucked up. We were too late. I gave you false hope when I should have let you mourn in peace," I say.

Lennox works his jaw, and a shadow falls over his face. His mind is instantly thrown back into the darkness of that night all over again.

"Iris is dead. I didn't find her before she was killed. I shouldn't have convinced you that I thought she was alive. Me and my stupid sunny disposition, with its overly hopeful sentiment fucked up. I should have never given you hope. She's gone, and the only thing we can do now is get revenge for her death."

Lennox sinks into a plush chair; his emotions suddenly void on his face.

Gage sits down on the nearby couch, but I remain standing. I have too much energy to sit.

"I know it doesn't mean much, but I'm sorry. I'm so sorry, Lennox," I beg.

Lennox's eyes jolt up, looking me dead in the eyes. "You're sorry?"

I flinch. He's about to beat my ass, and I'm going to let him. "More sorry than you could ever know."

He shakes his head and stands. "I meant, you have nothing to be sorry for. You didn't kill Iris. And she's probably been dead all these years. So there was no way to save her. Don't be sorry."

I swallow hard, but he's wrong if he thinks I shouldn't be sorry. And he's probably wrong that Iris died years ago instead of only weeks ago, but I don't tell him that. I don't tell him how close I came to finding her alive. How my involvement with the Retribution Kings, with Titus, with Lilith delayed my plans. If I didn't have such a split focus, then maybe I could have saved her in time.

Lennox walks over to the floor-to-ceiling window and stares out at the skyline. Even if she were alive, I'm not sure what bringing Iris back would do except complicate everything. He loved her, and now he loves Rialta. I don't know who he'd choose if she were alive.

But she could give him answers—closure. And maybe that would have been worth it.

"I should tell Rialta the truth," Lennox says as much to himself as to us.

"You can't," Gage and I say at the same time.

Lennox frowns, his jaw set, but he slowly nods as if he lost his mind for a second and said the wrong thing. He knows he can't say anything to her. Before I can remind him why, a pounding on the door draws our attention.

All three of us have our weapons drawn in an instant. Gage pulls out his phone to pull up the security cameras. He tenses before slowly turning the screen toward me.

Lilith and Titus stand outside the door, and Lilith looks like she's about to burn this building to the ground.

The corner of my lips lift at how adorable she looks when she's this pissed off. In another life, we could be together. In another life...

Lennox begins to lower his gun, but I shake my head. "I wouldn't do that if I were you."

He frowns. "I thought they were your friends. Why am I protecting her sisters if not?"

"It's complicated," is all I say as I stomp toward the door. My body tenses—I'm not in a place at all to deal with any of this.

"Hayes killed Lilith's dad," Gage says, filling Lennox in.

"Oh, shit," Lennox says.

I roll my eyes as I throw open the door, holding the gun at my side but ready to aim it at a moment's notice.

"Where are they?" Lilith asks, pushing her way into the room. I don't see any visible weapons on her but I know they are there. They are always there. I shouldn't underestimate her.

"Where are who?" I ask, watching as she searches Lennox's small apartment.

Titus steps in behind her, but doesn't say a word. I can't tell if he's her backup or bodyguard or jailor. Or if he plans on killing me just like Lilith does.

"My sisters," she spits out.

"They're not here, they're—" Lennox says.

But Lilith doesn't let him finish his sentence. She pulls out a dagger from the back pocket of her jeans and flings it at Lennox, barely missing his ear.

"Jesus," Lennox says, raising his hands with a small smirk on his lips. His eyes cut to me sympathetically for how much I have my hands full with this one.

I sigh. *Don't I know it...*

She runs at him, pulling another dagger I'm sure she'll

fling into Lennox's chest next. But I grab her arm and stop her before she has the chance.

She turns all her rage on me. She throws her arm back in a wide swing, before aiming for my upper chest.

I grab her wrist, stopping her from sinking the blade into my flesh. Anger flares in her eyes, but I keep my expression neutral. I can't let her know any of my emotions or even that I have any.

She spins, breaking free of my hold and slashing her knife across my bicep.

I aim my gun at her. "Stop this."

She laughs as if I'm holding a harmless puppy in my hands instead of a gun. A second later, she's kicked my gun to the floor, scooped it up in her hands, and aimed it at my head.

I don't move. I don't hold my hands up. I don't flinch.

She frowns.

"Fight me," she screams, her voice breaking as if she needs more of a fight.

"You win, murderous one."

She shakes her head. Her hand trembles, holding the gun. "That was no fight. You barely even tried."

I chuckle. "Now I don't even fight good enough for you."

She growls. "I hate you."

"I know." I glance around the room and notice it's empty except for the two of us.

"You going to kill me and live up to your name?" my eyes darken.

She grinds her teeth together. "Not until I learn why."

Suddenly, her face lights up, and she races past me. I turn in time to see her throw her arms around her sisters.

I sigh. She should have killed me.

CHAPTER 4

Lilith

I STROKE Adeline's hair as she sleeps in the bed with her head in my lap as I run my hand through her auburn hair. Her hair isn't nearly as red as Kennedy's and definitely not as red as my own fiery color.

"I'm so sorry," I say mindlessly, as I continue to stroke Adeline's hair, hoping that she sleeps through this conversation. She's only thirteen—too young to experience any trauma.

"I told you you have nothing to be sorry for," Kennedy says. Kennedy's eyes go to Adeline sleeping in my lap. We both envy her. She's too young to understand what happened.

"Tell me the truth. Did they hurt you?"

Kennedy doesn't look at me for a long moment. She just stares at Adeline. My heart jumps wildly in my chest. Lennox hurt them. Or one of his men. Or Hayes. If Hayes hurt them, I swear...

A sob wells in my throat, but I know I have to be strong for them. I was the one who put them in this situation. I was the one who trusted the wrong person. I should have known it wasn't safe. I should have hidden them away myself.

I'll never forgive myself. Whatever happened to them, I'll carry with me for the rest of my life. "Lilith, look at me," Kennedy says in a serious tone.

I blink back my tears and look at Kennedy.

"Nothing happened."

"What do you mean?"

"I mean, Lennox didn't hurt us. His men didn't hurt us. Hayes didn't hurt us."

My eyes widen as I stare at her, my hand slowly stopping stroking Adeline's hair.

"We were holed up in a hotel room with crappy internet, bad TV, and junk food. So if social isolation is torture, then yes, we were tortured." Kennedy tries to joke.

"You're telling the truth?"

"Yes, I wouldn't lie to you, not when it is about Adeline."

I look down at our younger sister's head as she sleeps deeply in my lap. If there's one thing we both agree on, we would both do anything to protect her innocence.

I study Kennedy for a moment longer, trying to decipher if she's hiding anything from me. Trying to see if the emotions she's feeling have anything to do with some trauma she just experienced. But I don't see anything out of the ordinary. Just the same old Kennedy.

My shoulders slump in relief, but I can't make sense of it. *Why did Lennox truly keep them safe? Why not use them against me? Why not torture them for information? Why not blackmail me or Titus or any of the Retribution Kings to get what they needed?*

I honestly don't know whose side anyone is on anymore. And I don't know who to trust. All I know is that I don't trust Hayes, and I shouldn't trust Titus either.

But I have to trust somebody. I can't keep my sister safe on my own. I have money now, but I don't have anyone to protect them, and hiring private security wouldn't be enough, especially now if I marry Titus, they will always have a mark on their backs, they will always be in danger, I have to find a way to protect them. Titus offered me a way, and it seems like it's the only choice.

"Spain or Italy?" I ask Kennedy.

"Neither," Kennedy spits out like I just asked her to choose whether she wants to live on the streets or in a jail cell instead of two countries where she can have an adventure with Adeline.

"What do you mean? Do you prefer a different country? Just say the word, and we'll figure it out."

"I mean, I'm not leaving you. I mean, you're not shipping me off to some foreign country."

"This is the best option. You got to start a new life with Adeline overseas. You'll forget this life. You'll forget me. And you'll be safe."

Kennedy shakes her head like I've lost my mind. "We're not leaving you."

"You did before."

"That was different, and you know it. It was temporary, and we could still see you if we chose to. This is permanent; you're faking our deaths, and we can never come back. We will almost certainly never see each other again. The answer is no."

I gently roll out from underneath Adeline. I tuck the covers over her and then motion for Kennedy to follow me out of the room.

Kennedy follows me closely behind, holding her arms across her chest. She gives me an aggressive glare. Clearly trying to tell me that she's not planning on changing her mind anytime soon.

"You're not thinking straight. You have to do this for Adeline."

"I know perfectly well how to keep Adeline safe, thank you very much. And she's not gonna leave you any more than I do."

I run my hand through my hair, not sure how to approach this with her, how to convince her. "Then, if you won't do this for Adeline, do this for yourself. You're seventeen, soon to be eighteen. You know what happens when you turn eighteen. You'll be initiated into the Retribution Kings you'll have no choice. Is that what you want? To become one of us? To have your life destroyed? Because trust me, initiation changes you, and you can never go back. You'll never be the sister you once were, the woman you once were. And I don't want that for you. I want you to be able to choose the life that you want for yourself. I don't want you to be forced into initiation. I don't want you to be forced to become a Retribution King."

"But it's ok that you're one?" Her eyebrows jump up, and her lips thin.

"If I had a choice, I wouldn't be; I would've found a different life."

"Bullshit. You were made for this life. Don't think I haven't noticed your training. Don't think I haven't noticed how skilled you are."

"Even so, I would want the choice. I didn't have that choice. It was taken from me, and I could've chosen to do any number of things with the skills that I have."

"Your skills could keep us safe. We have money now. We would be protected together."

"I can't keep you safe, and you know it."

Kennedy's eyes narrow at me as if she's trying to understand why I'm truly doing this. "Why are you doing this?"

"Doing what? Protecting you?"

"No, I mean, what is it costing you to keep us safe? If we do this, if we allow you to fake our deaths, if we run away and start a new life, what is it costing you?"

"Nothing," I lie.

"I don't believe you. What are they going to force you to do? Are you being forced to marry Titus? Is that the deal?"

"Nobody is forcing me to do anything, and nobody will force me to do anything ever again. I am marrying Titus because I want to."

"I don't believe you. You've never wanted to get married, and I've never heard you mentioning this Titus person before."

Before I can say anything, I hear heavy footsteps coming down the hallway. "There you are; you know I can't sleep without you in my bed." Titus approaches me, lifting my chin and kissing me tenderly like a couple in love. We haven't kissed before. It's the most affection either of us has displayed to each other, and I'm shocked that he did it. I'm shocked that he knew that Kennedy needed to see us as a normal couple together in order to go. It's just another way I owe him. Another way I am in debt to him, another trait he possesses that confuses me. *How can a man like Titus be so kind one minute and cruel the next? And which man is he really?*

Kennedy looks at us suspiciously as Titus drapes his arm around my shoulder, holding me tight against his body. I wrap my arms around his waist and lean into his chest, like it's the most natural thing in the world to be doing.

"I was just asking Kennedy where she would like to start her life over."

"And what did you decide?"

Kennedy looked us both over, and I'm not sure what

she's going to say. Is she going to continue to fight me, or is she going to give in to the plan and take Adeline far away, start a new life, and forget about me?

"I've always wanted to see Italy; we'll start there."

CHAPTER 5

Hayes

I STAND at the back of the church, looking down the aisle. The sanctuary is completely filled, not an open seat left. Tranquil music fills the room from the harpist, while my eyes continuously scan for any threats.

"See anything?" Gage asks.

"No," I answer simply.

"Are you sure you can handle this?" Gage asks.

"Don't ask me that again," I growl.

Gage's sigh fills the tiny radio in my ear. Gage is in charge of security, but Titus demanded I be here as his second and as his best man. Lilith wants me dead, but somehow I'm still breathing. The fact that Titus wants me here either means Lilith no longer cares about me, or he's going to have me killed as a wedding present for her. I don't really care if I live or die at the moment, though. All I care about is fixing what I royally fucked up before I die.

Lennox said he never really believed Iris was alive, but I know better. He had hope; we all did. Revenge is what I promised him now. Someone in this church was responsible for her death, and I'll get revenge for him today. Then I won't care if Lilith or Titus put a bullet between my eyes.

The music changes, the beat picking up to form a cheerful tune. And when I look to my left, Abigail is standing next to me in a fiery red dress, the same shade as Lilith's hair. My eyebrows jump at the sight of her not in a classic bridesmaid color, but this has Lilith written all over it.

"Can I trust you to walk me down the aisle, or are you going to try to trick me into getting into your bed, whore?" Abigail asks.

"You're not my type," I say, not even acknowledging the whore jab. I deserve it.

"I'm going to make you pay for hurting my best friend."

"You're going to have to get in line," I say drolly.

I lead Abigail down the aisle, taking in every man and woman's face as we walk. I look for any sign of someone here who may have hurt Iris, but every face is filled with disappointment. They want me gone. They think I don't belong with the Retribution Kings. They all want me dead.

Abigail and I part at the end of the aisle, taking our places in front of the altar. Next down the aisle are Kennedy and Adeline walking hand-in-hand. Titus doesn't have any other groomsmen—it's just me.

I study the two sisters as they walk toward me.

Adeline has a genuine look of joy on her face, but Kennedy eyes me suspiciously behind her clearly fake, broad smile. Both of them look gorgeous in their red dresses. With their shades of auburn hair curled on top of their heads, there is no doubt the sisters are just as strong-willed as Lilith.

They take their place next to Abigail, and the music shifts once again.

My eyes slide to the large wooden ornate doors that open once again at the end of the aisle. When they do, my jaw drops. Lilith and Titus make their entrance as all eyes shift to them. Silence stretches throughout the room as everyone takes in the sight of the couple. Titus is standing in a perfectly fitted sharp tux, but nobody is paying him any attention. All eyes are locked on the incredibly gorgeous woman next to him.

Lilith is wearing a full lace gown with bright red roses throughout, which match the shade of her bridesmaids' dresses. Her red hair is curled with just the right amount of wild, out-of-place strands to match her personality. A gold crown sits atop her red mane.

Together, they take a step down the aisle, and the slit on her dress rises up almost to her hip. A band wraps around her thigh, proudly displaying a dagger. They aren't hiding her. They aren't hiding how dangerous she is. They aren't hiding the fact that Titus plans to make her his queen. They are hiding nothing from the world.

For a moment, my heart clenches. This is exactly what she deserves, what they both deserve.

They walk with their heads held high, looking down at no one as they walk together hand in hand down the aisle.

They stop just in front of me and turn to face each other, their eyes staring deeply at each other. If anyone didn't know any better, they might think the look in their eyes is love. Myself, Gage, and maybe Kennedy are the few that know the truth. This isn't about love. This is about protection. This is about revenge. This is about an arrangement.

I can barely breathe as the minister starts speaking. This is what I did. *I did this.* They are getting married because of me. This is what I wanted.

My heart tears apart in my chest, ripping into me for causing it so much pain. Despite my job, despite doing the right thing when it came to Lilith, my heart has never been so broken.

Vows are exchanged. Rings are placed. Then, the minister steps away, and Titus faces the crowd.

"Lilith has already been initiated into the Retribution Kings. She has already gone through another initiation to become my wife. But Lilith Hart, do you swear to be a loyal Retribution King from this point forward? To always be loyal to us, no matter what? To always be loyal to me and our vows above all?" Titus says.

"I do," Lilith replies with a fire in her voice. She knows the consequence of breaking this vow is death.

"Lilith is now my wife. She is my queen. She is just as much a leader of the Retribution Kings as I am. And every one of you here will follow her as you do me. You will protect her as you do me."

"We will," the crowd says. Titus glares at them all, promising them a long and painful death if they don't uphold the vow.

The crowd erupts into cheers, welcoming her easily as their new queen. But then again, they all know what she's been through to get to this point. They know what the initiation cost her. And that's what we all live by—initiation.

Initiation is the cost we all pay. It's the vow we all make. It's the promise that even in death, we will be loyal to the Retribution Kings.

"And now I claim you as my wife," Titus says before dipping her in his arms and landing his mouth on hers in a flaming hot kiss.

I watch as her eyes close, accepting the kiss. I watch as her tongue lashes back against his in equal measure. I watch as her arms tighten around his neck. And when he brings her back up, I watch the gleam in her eyes. I can't tell if it's one of lust, or revenge, or of the arrangement they made together. But the look scares me nonetheless.

Music fills through the room, as do the hoops and

hollers from the crowd. Titus takes Lilith's hand in his, and they start running down the aisle.

Abigail, Kennedy, and Adeline chase after them.

I take my time walking down the aisle alone. It shouldn't feel so strange; I'm always alone. I will die with no woman on my arm. And that's how I like it.

Brief static buzzes in my earpiece, and Gage's heavy breathing tells me he's about to speak.

"Don't," I say, and the static vanishes.

I hear the crowd's happy footsteps behind me as they all follow to wish the happy couple well. I don't know if the traditional wedding night will be held. I don't know if Titus will need witnesses to the marital act tonight, but I can't think about that. I can't let my mind go there, or I'll never stop thinking about it—over and over and over.

Cars are lined up outside of the church to take Titus and Lilith, along with the bridal party, to the hotel where the reception is to be held. But before we even take one step towards the cars, gunfire erupts.

"Gage," I shout.

"Get them in the cars," he says calmly back.

Titus has Lilith covered, so I go for her sisters and friend. I shove them into the back of the nearest car, practically throwing them in, and tap the window, shouting at the driver to go.

I pull my gun out, looking for the threat. Gage's eyes meet mine as he runs around the corner of the church, looking frantic. He's never frantic; he's always the calm one. *Why is this different?*

An explosion sends us both flying in the air.

Fuck.

When we land and turn around, reality hits us hard. The car I just sent her sisters and friend in is now a ball of fire. Ash and smoke begin to rain down on us.

I'm in shock and white as a ghost, but Lilith's screams shake me from my stupor.

I can hear Lilith's agony above everything else. Above the gunfire, the screams of the crowd, the blaze of the fire. The heartbreak I hear in her voice is like nothing I've ever heard. And I've heard heartbreak. I've seen it up close, experienced it myself, but nothing like this.

She's going to run toward the car and try to save anyone inside, but I can't let her. No matter how painful it will be for her to not go, she can't put herself in harm's way.

She starts running, but I'm faster, and I tackle her to the ground.

"Let me go," she tries to shake free.

"No, go with Titus." My weight presses down on her, pinning her down. She's too shattered to realize she's strong enough and smart enough to find a way out of my hold.

She reaches for her dagger, and I have no doubt I'll let her take her anger out on me. She lifts the knife to my throat with a shaky hand as my body holds her to the ground.

"Kill me if it'll make you feel better, but either way, you aren't taking a step closer to that car."

"Fuck you," she says through heavy tears.

Titus and Gage are at my side a second later.

"Go with Titus, and I'll do everything I can to save your sisters." She stares at me with a heavy gaze I can't quite interpret.

"Go, I promise," I plead.

I don't know what she sees in my eyes, but she gently nods her head.

I stand up, pulling her with me and not letting go of her arms until Titus has a grip on her. The second I release her, I run to the car, knowing Gage will ensure Titus and Lilith get somewhere safe.

Ash burns my arms and face before I even reach the car.

The blaze has engulfed every inch of the car now, and the billowing smoke is heavy and thick.

I know…I know they're gone. I know it before I've even begun my search. But I don't let that stop me. I promised. And beyond the promise—they were innocent. They didn't deserve to die. They have to live.

I have to try for her. I promised. The words are all I think about as I circle the car—once, twice, three times. I get close enough that the flames whip at my face and burn my cheeks and hands. My throat begins to close up as a violent cough wrecks through my body.

They're gone. Once again, I was too late. Once again, I couldn't save anyone. Once again, Lilith is going to want me dead.

CHAPTER 6

Lilith

I PACE back and forth in the honeymoon suite, while Titus and Gage stare at me silently. Gage is sitting on the couch while Titus is leaning against the door frame. With his tux jacket gone, his tie hanging loosely around his neck, and the top buttons of his shirt undone, Titus watches me closely, afraid I might truly break.

But he's the only one who knows the truth.

My sisters and Abigail are currently on a flight to Italy, and soon they'll be safe. It means I'll never see them again, but that's the price I'll pay. The plan didn't include Abigail initially, but after talking to her on the phone about my wedding, I realized she needed a way out, too. So I made her the same offer, and she accepted.

My bare feet hit the scratchy carpet over and over again. I can feel the rough fabric, every crumb and imperfection on the sole of my foot as I pace. This hotel room may be expensive, but the flooring still feels cheap. It's probably because most people don't pace back and forth barefoot in their hotel room and complain about how scratchy the carpet is.

I don't have to fake my anxiety. It floods through me hard and fast, a gushing river of stress that won't calm down until I know they're safe. Until then, I have to put on a show, and so does Titus.

Gage doesn't know the truth. From his actions, he doesn't seem suspicious either. He truly thinks we were attacked, and my sisters and friend are most likely gone. But still, he hasn't said any of that to me. He lets me have hope that they survived.

"Come here," Titus says.

I shake my head at him. If I stop pacing, stop letting anxiety flow through me, and let his arms wrap around me, I might actually relax. It's something someone wouldn't do when they just saw the car their family was riding in explode.

Titus frowns, but he doesn't push the issue. I don't know if I can trust him, but I don't have a choice. I made a deal with him to ensure my family's safety. I'm putting all of my trust in him because he's the only one who can keep my family safe. He's the only one that can help me get the revenge I need.

And after? I haven't let myself think that far ahead. Maybe I'll be able to change the Retribution Kings as Titus's wife. Maybe I'll find some purpose again. Maybe I'll grow to like Titus, like he says I will. But I won't fall in love, never again.

There's a rough knock on the door, forceful enough to know the person on the other side of the door doesn't come with good news.

I freeze, stopping mid-pace.

Gage runs to the door and throws it open, as if he's the one waiting for the information about his sisters and not me. I already know who's standing in the doorway, but I'm terrified to look him in the eye.

When Titus and I made this plan, I didn't think Hayes

would play so heavily into it. I had no idea he would tackle me to the ground to prevent me from injuring myself in the fire. I had no idea that he would personally be the one to search for my sisters and friend in the aftermath, and I don't know how to feel about that.

When my head finally turns toward Hayes, I'm not prepared for what I see. I can barely make him out beneath the ash and burns on his skin. He's still wearing his tux pants, but his white undershirt is now covered in black soot. His glasses are gone, most likely broken. His hair is disheveled, no longer in the man bun I'm used to him wearing, and completely tangled with sweat and ashes.

But it's the burns on his skin that draw my attention the most. There are scorch marks on his cheeks, forehead, and forearms.

My mouth drops slightly, and my eyes widen—he really did search for them. He really did everything possible to try to find them for me. He really did have hope that he could pull them out of that fire.

Foolish, stupid, hopeful man. My sunshine in the darkest of hours. And a fucking liar.

Hayes looks at me, his expression blank, and the corner of his eyes wrinkled in lines of exhaustion. This day was heavy for him, too.

His eyes cut to Titus for a moment, as if to tell him the truth first before he tells me. Titus walks over to me and intertwines his fingers through mine, preparing for my inevitable collapse.

Hayes takes a couple of steps into the hotel suite, looking me directly in the eyes.

I don't have to fake my reaction. The look of devastation on his face hits me like a truck. My body trembles, my eyes water, and a sob bubbles up in my throat.

"No," I croak out. "No, no, no..."

"They're gone," Hayes says simply and quietly.

A cry rips through my body, exploding with a force I'm sure every person in the hotel heard. I fall to my knees, trembling and burying my head in my hands as the tears fall and fall and fall.

They're gone. Those words can never be more true. They're gone, even if they're not dead.

I feel Titus's hand rubbing my back in slow, gentle circles. The room is silent except for my cries, and I can feel all three men staring at me.

Finally, I look up at Hayes. "Who?"

"I'm sorry, but I don't know," he replies.

I grind my teeth together, my nostrils flaring. My whole body shifts from grief to uncontrollable rage. "The Corsi mafia? Lennox? Was this his doing?"

"No—I know you don't believe a word out of my mouth anymore, but trust me when I say this wasn't him. I don't know who it was, and I won't rest until I do, until I'm able to give you the revenge you need. But it wasn't him, and it wasn't me. I would never hurt you that way," Hayes says.

His voice is so sincere, so honest, so raw. He's acting—he has to be doing the same thing I am. He did it once before, and he's doing it again now. He's acting like he cares about my sisters and friend, acting like he cares about me.

"I don't believe you," I snap at him, lifting myself to my feet.

"Lilith, I think he's telling the truth," Titus says.

"Lennox would never do this," Gage chimes in.

I shake my head. "I don't believe you," I growl at Hayes.

I shove him in the chest. "I don't believe that you did everything possible to rescue my sisters and friend. I don't believe that you care they're dead. I don't believe you at all." Even though every mark on his body tells the story of how hard he tried to find them, to save them, to bring them back to me, I push through all of that and let my anger explode through my body.

"I hate you," I whisper.

"It was my fault," he says.

I cock my head in confusion, my eyes turning vicious. He's goading me, trying to get me to fight him once again, and I let him. I attack without finesse, throwing all my training out the window.

He should've been able to block my punch, but he doesn't. He lets me hit him hard in the jaw, his head whipping to the side as his raw, burnt flesh crumples under my fist.

I almost wince at the pain he must be in, but my fury is too much. This man destroyed me more than any man ever has. He took my father from me. He stole my heart and broke it. I'll never forgive him—ever.

I attack quickly and relentlessly, throwing everything I have into it. Punch, kick, spin. Attack, attack, attack. He doesn't fight back. He doesn't even block me. He lets every punch, every kick land on his body.

I spin, sweeping his legs out from under him as I grab my dagger at my thigh and thrust it down over his heart, stopping just as the tip nicks his skin.

"Do it," he says.

I shake my head. "You have such a death wish. Why? Why do you wanna die by my hand so badly?"

He doesn't answer me.

"I'm not going to kill you, not tonight. You don't deserve an easy death. You have to live with what you did first."

As I sheath my dagger, I'm surprised Gage didn't try to stop me. Titus didn't pretend to try to stop me, either.

Gage doesn't seem afraid of me killing his friend at all. He just watches me closely, too closely.

I ease off Hayes and turn toward Titus. I don't know exactly why I know what to do next to hurt Hayes. He's a liar, but he wears his feelings out in the open. He cares about me, maybe still even wants me. And if I can't kill him tonight, I'll cause him some more pain any way I can.

I wrap my arms around Titus's neck and kiss him passionately and aggressively.

"I need you. I need you to make me forget. I need you to take away the pain. I need you to help me grieve," I moan to Titus.

Titus looks down at me sadly, knowing what this will cost me. "We don't have to do anything," he says.

"We do—I want to. I want to consummate our marriage. I need you."

I turn my head to Gage. "Get out."

Gage nods and silently leaves, as if he can't get out of here fast enough. He accepts my order as if it was from Titus.

Then I look directly at Hayes with a wicked gleam in my eyes. *I know your secret.* He still cares. Maybe even his feelings were real, and he did love me, but it didn't stop him from following orders and fucking me over.

So, I plan to do the same to him.

"Sit here and guard the door. You don't want to know the wrath you will feel if you leave your post or let anyone through that door tonight," I say to Hayes.

Then I pull Titus into the bedroom, kissing him roughly and glancing at Hayes from the corner of my eye. This will be the worst punishment possible for him. He'll listen to Titus fuck me, while his skin burns from trying to rescue my sisters and friend.

Hayes is a liar—he fucking cares about me. I don't know how deeply. I don't understand him at all. I still hate him for what he did—for killing my father, for lying to me. But as I shut the door on his face, my heart whispers to me—*liar*. Hate isn't the strongest emotion I feel toward Hayes.

CHAPTER 7

Lilith

THE SOUND of the door closing echoes through the room. I turn the lock on the door, and I can barely breathe. *What am I doing? Why the hell did I think this was a good idea?* My heart is throbbing in my chest. *I can't fuck Titus. I can't actually go through this, can I?*

I rest my hand on the door for a second, wishing I could feel Hayes through the door. Then I remember everything he's put me through. Anger flourishes inside me, as my heart turns to steel.

I will do this. I will make him pay. And I will learn the truth.

My eyes cut to Titus to see him standing in the bedroom with his hands in his pockets. This is more than just revenge. This is my new life. I married Titus. There is no getting out of that; the Retribution Kings will never let me. I made a vow, and I know what is expected of me tonight.

Titus eyes me cautiously, unsure if I laid a trap for Hayes or him. He chose me for my skill set; at least, that's what he tells me. He's not afraid of me, and I'm not afraid of him, but right now, our respective stares aren't so sure.

"We don't have to do this," Titus mouths silently to me.

"We do," I mouth back.

Titus's eyes darken as he rakes his eyes up and down my body.

"Like what you see?" I tease, whispering.

I know he does as his eyes take in every inch of my pale skin marked in white and red lace.

He nods gently.

I smile, forcing myself to try and enjoy this. The only way I have a chance of doing that is to stop talking, stop thinking, and take everything from Titus, just as he'll take everything from me.

I grab him forcefully, wrapping my arms around his neck and going in for a punishing kiss. His lips meet mine, kissing me as roughly as I'm kissing him. I moan, purposely letting the sound escape my throat. The kiss is fine, but it's not moan-worthy. But tonight I am going to be as loud as fucking possible. I want Hayes to hear everything. I want him to realize what he gave up. I want him to realize what he could've had but decided to throw it all away by lying to me.

Titus catches my wrists in his hands, pulling them gently from his neck and tugging my lips from his mouth. He tilts his head towards the bathroom, motioning for me to follow him, and releases my wrists.

I moan again as I watch Titus walk away from me toward the bathroom. The moan is exasperated and exhausted, but it's real. After everything I went through today, the moan is perfect.

After I enter the bathroom, Titus closes the door gently and turns on the faucet.

"What?" I ask a little too snappily, but I need him to be a willing participant as much as I am. It's not like we have a choice. The Retribution Kings expect us to consummate our marriage and produce an heir.

"Come here," he says gently.

I step toward him, stopping when I feel his hot breath against my cheek. Titus turns towards my face and pulls a washcloth from under the sink. He wets it before cupping my chin and rubbing the washcloth against my face.

I look at myself in the mirror and realize I have mascara and makeup smeared all over my face. Titus is so gentle as he wipes it away, so kind, so caring. When he's finished, I stare up at him with wide eyes. Titus really is a good man. If I could ever get past Hayes, then maybe I could learn to love Titus. And if not love him, then maybe we could figure out a way for us both to be happy together.

But as Titus looks down at me, it's like he can read my mind, and I can read his. It doesn't matter how kind he is. It doesn't matter how hard I try to make this relationship work. This isn't what we want. This isn't want either of us want, not really. I loved another man, and it damn near killed me. I won't go through that again. And Titus has secrets of his own; it's clear he won't be sharing in this moment.

He doesn't ask me again if I'm sure, if I really want to go through this. He just turns off the faucet and then captures my lips with his as he begins to back me out of the bathroom.

Titus's hands cling to my hips, and mine return to his neck as I slip my tongue between his lips. I want to enjoy this. I want to enjoy tonight. I *need* to enjoy tonight.

My hand slips up, reaching into his hair and tangling with it as I deepen the kiss.

His hair is thick and soft beneath my grasp—but it's not Hayes. It's not his long, thick hair I can run my fingers fully through. It's not his man bun that I can grip. Titus's cheeks are smooth, unlike Hayes's rough stubble. I feel safe in Titus's arms, but I don't feel the thick, corded muscles of

Hayes holding onto me. I don't feel those arms around me telling me he'll never let me go, telling me to trust him because he knows exactly how to work my body.

Fuck.

Although Titus is kissing me, and his hands are on my hips, he doesn't move to take things further, not like Hayes would. Hayes would already be pushing the limits of my body. He would already know my needs before I even realize them myself. He's knows my body better than anybody. Titus is a kind man, but he doesn't know me. I'm not sure he ever will.

It's up to me to push things further. The man on the other side of the wall is what drives me. I bite at Titus's lip, pulling a growl from his body.

I grin against his lips.

"You're a vicious little thing, aren't you?" he says.

"You've only just begun to see how vicious I can be," I say seductively.

Titus chuckles, but it's not a real laugh. It's not one that has me laughing along with him. My face is still serious, and I suspect I'll never truly laugh again.

I pull out the knife attached to my thigh, and Titus's eyes dilate. His eyebrows jump ever so slightly as if he's afraid I'll use the knife on him.

I laugh manically as I toss the knife at the wall. The knife goes into the wall with a sharp thud.

"I chose my wife well," Titus says.

"Tonight, I'm all yours. I'll fulfill any fantasy; do anything you want," I say, letting my voice drop into a lust-filled purr.

Titus doesn't breathe. For a moment, I think this is just as hard and new for him as it is for me. He's not the ruthless leader that past Retribution Kings leaders were. At least he's not that way when it comes to his women.

"Unbutton me," I command. I turn around, brushing my hair to one side and exposing my back to him.

Titus wordlessly does as I command. I feel his strong fingers against my back, working the buttons down, down, down until he reaches the last one at the top curve of my ass.

As he finishes the last button, I pull the straps off my shoulders and shimmy the lace dress down my body until it's a puddle on the floor. I'll give it to Titus. He really did let me choose my own wedding dress. This dress was all me. And I'll miss feeling that beautiful. I suspect I'll never feel this beautiful ever again.

I turn and face him completely nude except for the tiara on top of my head. The dress was so tight there was no need for undergarments.

Titus's eyes look at me with lust as he takes in my gentle curves. My pale skin is marked with freckles, and my red curls bounce at the swell of my breasts.

"Jesus, woman," he groans.

"My turn," I say, grabbing his shirt and yanking hard enough that all his buttons fly apart with one pull.

He tilts his head down to kiss me tenderly, but I don't waste any time undoing the buttons and zipper of his pants and yanking them down his thighs, until his cock springs free. I don't study it closely, other than to note it's thick and large. But it's not Hayes's pierced cock. It's not the cock that I would have done anything for, the cock that filled me so completely.

Our lips never leave each other, and I let every sound free —every moan, every growl, every whimper. The roughness of my kisses pulls lust-filled noises from him as well. We're loud, so fucking loud. For a moment, I forget why we need to be loud. I get lost in the frenzy, forgetting what has to happen next. The kisses are nice, and I'm sure the sex will be too. But it's not...

I clear my mind, not allowing myself to go there again. This is vengeance, sure, but I also deserve to enjoy this. Titus is a good-looking man, and I'm sure he knows just how to handle me in the bedroom.

I pull us onto the bed—me completely naked and Titus still partially covered in his shirt and pants. I don't think as I reach for his hardness between his legs. I need him to fuck me now before I think too much about this and tell him to stop.

The growl that leaves him is loud and uncontrolled. It's pure lust.

Good, he wants this. I can feel how hard he is in my hand, how ready he is.

"Fuck me, Titus."

He nestles between my legs, not bothering to explore any other part of my body. He seems to also know that we need to do this now before either of us realizes how bad of an idea it is, how dangerous of a game we're playing.

I feel his tip at my entrance. I'm slick and ready for him.

I want this.

He wants this.

"Do it," I whisper.

He's right there with me. He begins to thrust but then stops at the last second. Something torn marks his features. Something dark, something secret, and I know he won't do this. I don't know why. I don't know what holds him back.

A scream rips through me out of utter frustration and anguish.

Something slams into the door, and Titus reaches for his gun at the back of his waistband. He uses his body to shield me from the soon-to-be intruder.

Another thud hits the door, and it bursts open. Hayes runs inside, his gun drawn and aimed at Titus. Titus's gun is aimed right at Hayes's heart. But Hayes isn't looking at Titus or his gun. He's looking at me with real fear in his eyes.

Hayes thought Titus was hurting me. He thought my scream was one of real pain instead of frustration. He cares. I swear I see a flicker of love and pain in Hayes's eyes at the sight of Titus on top of my naked body. My lips curl up in a wicked grin. Hayes may have won the previous rounds, but I won this one.

CHAPTER 8

Hayes

I STOP outside the door of Titus's office, my heart thundering in my chest. This is the last place I want to be right now.

It's been a week since Titus and Lilith got married. One week I've spent searching for any clue as to who killed her sisters and friend. One week I've put my own mission to find Iris's killer on hold. One week I've been obsessed with doing something right for Lilith, anything to offset all the pain she's endured. But I'm no closer to finding out who killed her sisters and friend than I was the moment it happened.

I knock rapidly on the door and wait to hear Titus welcome me in before opening it. I half expect Lilith to be naked, their lips locked together, and bare bodies thrusting, taunting me like she did the night of their wedding.

What I find in his office is much worse. They're sitting in chairs, side-by-side with their fingers interlocked, looking at each other with warmth in their eyes. It can only be described as the beginning of love.

My legs falter for just a moment, but quickly, I force my signature smile to my face and greet them relaxedly. I don't know how they grew so close so quickly. Shared trauma does that to people, though, I guess.

"Take a seat, Hayes. We have much to discuss," Titus says.

Taking a seat across from them, I smile at them both. "It's good to see you two enjoying married life and not trying to kill each other."

Titus chuckles. "Oh, my dear Lilith has definitely tried to kill me a time or two. But I don't hold that against her. In fact, it's a turn-on."

It's definitely a turn-on.

Lilith is dressed in all-black, head to toe. Dark black jeans caress her thighs and hips while a long-sleeve black shirt hugs her firm stomach and curvy breasts. Her hair is pulled up in a messy bun of red curls on top of her head. Despite everything that's happened to her over the past week, she looks stronger than ever. Except for some puffiness under her eyes, you'd never know what she went through this week.

Her fierce appearance is almost as if she spent the entire week honing her skills instead of crying alone in her bedroom. I would expect nothing less from her, but she still shouldn't have to mourn any more family members. It's not fair. This world has taken everything from her. I've taken everything from her. But if she's truly happy with Titus, then maybe I gave her something. For once, I made the right decision.

I stare at their interlinked fingers and watch as Titus rubs his thumb gently back and forth across her palm. They are both so at ease with each other, like they've known each other their whole lives instead of merely weeks.

"So, have you brought me here to kill me or torture me?" I ask teasingly.

"So eager to die," Lilith says, her first words to me.

"I'm just here to serve. I'm a loyal Retribution King. Whatever you desire, I shall do," I say.

"Glad to hear it, because I have a new mission for you," Titus says. He glances over at Lilith, searching her face for something before looking back at me.

"You are to be Lilith's bodyguard," Titus says.

My jaw drops, and my breath catches in my throat. Of all the things I thought they might ask of me—this wasn't even on my radar. I thought they would ask me to hunt Lilith's sisters' killer. I thought they might ask me to relinquish my role as second or do some dirty work. I thought they might whore me out again and again as punishment for killing Lilith's father. I thought they'd torture me somehow until she was finally ready to kill me herself. Until she let go of the heartache I caused her and that tiny morsel of love she felt towards me before I betrayed her.

"You want me to be Lilith's bodyguard?" I ask in disbelief.

"Yes," they say together.

My eyes roll back and forth between the two of them, trying to find some sign that this is a joke. Lilith can't possibly trust me to be her bodyguard. I know Titus trusts me with his life, but I don't know how they expect me to do this. I don't know how they expect me to listen to them fuck night after night. I can barely handle watching them hold hands.

"You will be her bodyguard. You will protect her with your life. You will do everything she tells you to—no questions asked. And I mean everything and anything. She has equal power to me. You'll report directly to her. She determines if you're doing your job well or not. You will never leave her side," Titus continues.

"This is the debt I require of you. You killed my father, and so you owe me a life. This is how you will repay me.

And maybe if you do your job well, I'll decide to spare your life and let you live," Lilith says.

"Can you agree to those terms? Will you vow to protect Lilith with your life? To be her willing servant in every way?" Titus asks.

I look at Lilith with a serious glimmer in my eyes. "Yes, I will protect you with my life. I vow to be your willing servant in every way. I vow to follow your every command. I vow to be eternally yours."

Lilith's eyes lock on mine, and her jaw tightens, as if it's painful for her to hear me say the words.

"Good, that's settled. I have a meeting I have to get to with the other Retribution King leaders. I'll leave you two to discuss the next steps," Titus says as he stands. He leans over and kisses Lilith gently on the lips, then leaves us alone in his office.

Neither of us move. We sit in our respective chairs, staring at each other. We both have so many secrets. There are so many emotions between us, but neither of us is willing to speak openly.

"Seems like you and your husband are getting along well," I say, my voice dripping with a sharp jealousy I didn't intend.

A wry smile curls up her lips. "Titus and I are perfect together. I should really thank you for that." Her eyes darken with rage, and she pulls a knife from a pocket on her thigh. She starts spinning it around, twiddling with it mindlessly. This is all a game to her. She's taunting me, letting me know I'm one flick of her wrist away from dying with her knife deep into my heart. She wouldn't miss, and I would deserve it.

"Be careful with Titus," I say quietly.

Her eyebrows raise. "That's your great advice? You work for the man. You set this up. You forced me into his arms and then got my sisters killed. You don't get to give me advice—not anymore."

I sigh and rub my hand on the back of my neck, trying to release the tension there.

"What, no jokes? No teasing? Where is the man who used to be all sunshine and roses?"

"That man was a lie," I say solemnly.

She nods slowly as if she understands now. "I see. Well, figure out how to bring him back because I'm not going to have a constant grump for a bodyguard. Sulking is my job. Yours is to try and make me happy."

I cock my head, turning on a smile. "I hope you and Titus learn some new moves soon. It's going to get really boring for me listening to the two of you fuck in missionary every night."

She glares at me.

"What? Can't take a joke?" I howl with laughter, my chuckle lacing the pain in my body and making me feel numb. I don't know how I ended up in this position. I don't know what life choices led me to this very dark place, but I regret all of them.

She smiles wickedly in my direction. "Your jokes could use some finesse, and you'd be wise not to joke about my husband. He and I could have you killed for what you've done to me, but I appreciate you trying." She rises from her chair.

I stand as well, trying to shift into bodyguard mode. This task would be much better suited for Gage. He's better at protecting. As she said, I'm better at making jokes and fucking everything up.

"Pack a bag; we leave in an hour," she says.

My brow furrows. "Leave for where exactly?"

"We are going to find The Abyss."

I freeze. "The Abyss has hunted Rialta her whole life. He

attacked the Retribution Kings. Lennox spent obscene amounts of time, money, and men trying to find him only to fail. The Abyss is a ruthless killer. You can't be serious?"

"I am."

"Why? Do you think they had something to do with your sisters' and friend's deaths?"

"It doesn't matter why. I don't have to explain myself to you. We are leaving in an hour; that's all you need to know." She starts to walk toward the door, but I cut her off. She slams into my hard body with a thud.

"If I'm to do my job well and protect you, then I need to know the facts. Why are we going? Do you even know where The Abyss is?"

"You don't need to know anything more than what I tell you." She pants against my neck, and I take a deep breath of her sharp scent. It fills my nostrils and taunts me. She's not mine. I can't touch her. Titus would kill me if I did.

"Why are we going to find The Abyss?" I say again, slowly, holding my breath as I do to avoid her scent.

"It's none of your concern." She lifts the knife now, dragging it over my chest, but I don't back down.

"Everything to do with you is my concern. You're up to something, or Titus has put you up to something. Tell me. I only want to protect you."

She shakes her head. "I don't trust you. I'll never trust you ever again."

"Then why choose me as your bodyguard? If you don't think I can protect you, then you wouldn't have chosen me."

I grab her wrist and disarm her, before yanking her hard to my body. She can't move in this position, and she's not strong enough to overpower me. But with us this close, she can feel exactly what her body does to me. My body betrays me, hardening against her, begging her for a second chance.

She smirks. "I don't need a bodyguard, and it's not about my protection. I plan to use you, to make you pay for everything you've ever done to me. And when my mission is over, I'll decide what torture you deserve next. You are mine to play with, Hayes. You're a fun plaything until I grow tired of you and decide that your death is more fun than your punishment."

She thrashes against my hold and snorts a laugh.

"You think Titus will save you because you are friends? Because you've been loyal to him? Because he trusts you? I don't trust you. You fucked up when you ensured my marriage to Titus. He made me as powerful as him. And I plan on wielding every drop of power I can to avenge my father's death, my sisters, and my friend. I will punish every person who ever hurt me," she says.

"And when you're done getting revenge, what then?"

She swallows hard. "Then, I'll learn to live with all I've lost."

I nod, releasing her. I don't tell her that going after The Abyss is a mistake. It won't solve any of her problems. Getting revenge won't bring back any of the people she loves. *But who am I to talk when my own mission now revolves around getting revenge for my friend?*

"One hour," she says, walking out the door, leaving me with no choice but to chase her. I follow begrudgingly, hoping I can figure out what her true goal is before we both end up dead.

CHAPTER 9

Hayes

I SWING A HASTILY PACKED bag over my shoulder and run out of my room to meet Lilith as quickly as possible. I'm not sure what she's up to, but I'm going to find out. I take one step into the hallway before my body slams into Gage's.

He glares at me with his dark brown eyes, already disapproving of whatever I'm about to do. He knows—he always knows. I don't know how he found out. *Was he listening? Did Titus tell him? Or did he find out via some other means?*

"They can't find out the truth," Gage says.

"I know," I growl back at him.

Gage grabs my bicep, preventing me from moving past him. "You leaving won't help us to find Iris's killer. It won't help us get our revenge."

"Maybe it will. Maybe I'm not cut out to do my part of the job. I failed enough. Maybe it's best if you and Lennox finish the job without me."

Gage shakes his head slowly. "We need you."

I want to disagree and tell him I'm just a fuck up. My head is spinning, and I don't know how to solve any of my own problems, let alone our group's. But I don't say anything.

"You should convince Lilith to stay. Going after The Abyss is not going to help her get revenge for her sisters and friend. He had nothing to do with their deaths."

"I know," I groan.

"Then convince her to stay and find the real killer here. Going after The Abyss is just going to get her killed."

"First of all, I can't convince Lilith of anything, not anymore. And second of all, I won't let anything happen to Lilith."

Gage's hard eyes see right through me. He can see through all of my lies, my half-truths, and everything I've done up to this point, but he doesn't call me out on my bull-shit. He doesn't force me to open my heart to him, or to tell him my own truth. We've all been through enough together that he knows I'll tell him in my own time.

"So what are you going to do?" He asks.

"I'm going to figure out why Lilith wants to go after The Abyss. There has to be a reason. As far as I know, she's never even heard of The Abyss until now. Why him? What is she up to? I plan on figuring it out."

Gage nods slowly, releasing my bicep. "Stay alive. We need you."

"You don't—you can get revenge without me."

"Maybe, but that's not why I said to stay alive. We need you. Beckett, River, Lennox, Rialta, and me—we all need you. So don't go get yourself killed trying to play a hero or a martyr."

I scoff. "When have I ever played the martyr?"

"All the fucking time. Stop thinking of yourself as less than."

"I have to go." I brush past Gage.

"You deserve her. If that's what you want, then figure out a way to have her."

I shake my head. "Lilith is exactly where she belongs. She's safe, protected. And Titus is a good man. Besides, I think they're starting to fall for each other." *She'd never fall for me, not now.*

Gage opens his mouth and then closes it, deciding better of saying whatever he was going to say.

"Don't fuck up," is what he says instead.

"I won't." And then I head out to meet Lilith, feeling like I'm about to fuck everything up.

———

I take my seat on the plane next to Lilith, still not having a clue of what we're doing exactly or why we're going to New York City. I'm especially confused because I know The Abyss isn't there, but I don't say it. Neither of us has spoken a word since we left for the airport. We don't speak as we buckle into our seats. We don't speak as we take off.

"Are you going to tell me why we're going to New York?" I finally ask her when I can no longer stand it.

She doesn't look up from the book in her lap. "No."

Sigh. I need to come up with a different way to get the truth out of her. I am not getting off this plane without knowing something.

I snatch the book off her lap and start reading the page she was on aloud.

"His eyes darkened, and a growl escaped his lips." I smile, my eyes cutting to hers. "I didn't take you for a romance book girl."

She snatches the book back. "Well, I am. And stop taking my shit and let me read in silence or..."

"Or you'll stab me? I know you don't have a knife on

you—security, and all that. So I'm pretty sure I'm safe, at least until we land."

She narrows her eyes at me. There's a bit of gleam in her eyes, enough to make me think she found a way to get a knife through security.

I chuckle. "So sly and conniving, murderous one. Still, I'm pretty sure I'm safe, at least until we land." I place my arms behind my head and lean my seat back, relaxing as if she doesn't unnerve every part of my body.

"You should have a weapon on you, too, since you're supposed to be my bodyguard," she says.

"I don't need a weapon to protect you."

Her eyes scan mine instead of her book. "I'm not telling you anything, so use your charms on someone else."

"I'm just doing my job and trying to protect you like you want. You told me to return to my true self, and this is my true self." I let my eyes run up and down her body, dragging slowly over my favorite parts of her.

She blushes. "Knock it off."

"I can't look at you?"

"No."

I laugh, and I swear I see a tug in the corner of her lips. She wants to laugh, to smile, but her annoyance with me wins out. She gives me nothing. *And what do I expect from a woman grieving the loss of her family?* This is the only way to make any progress with her. There's never a wrong time to make her laugh or smile.

"So, tell me more about you and Titus," I say.

"Well, he's a better kisser than you. A better lover, too. And he doesn't lie to me. So I'd say overall, he's a much better choice than you," her voice is dripping with spite. But I'm just glad she's talking. I figured she would bury her face in her book and ignore me for the rest of the flight.

"I'm sure he lies to you. All men lie, and especially men in a position like Titus."

Lilith closes her book, giving me her full attention. "Titus doesn't lie to me. He told me everything about his life. Everything that led to him becoming the leader of the Retribution Kings. Everything about what his goals are, who his enemies are, and why he chose me to be his wife. He even told me why he chose you to be his second."

"I didn't think you were so gullible, murderous one," I reply.

"I'm not. You erased that from me."

"Then why do you believe him so easily? You barely know the guy. He could be lying to you as easily as I was. He was the one that put me up to it, after all."

She grinds her teeth together. "I know Titus's role in putting you up to your job. I know what he did, and I know why. He wasn't the one warming my bed every night in a lie."

I shook my head. "So you'll forgive him, but not me?"

"If all you did was lie to me about loving me, then yes, I could've forgiven you—eventually. But that's not all you lied about, is it? You killed my father, and you still won't tell me why. Was he your enemy? Did he know some secret about you? Was it not personal, and the Retribution Kings forced you to kill him? Was it part of the initiation?"

I stare down on my lap, no longer meeting her gaze. I wish I could tell her the truth. She deserves to know the truth of how her father died and why. But I won't tell her— not now, maybe not ever. Maybe not even to save my own life.

She shakes her head with a sigh. Angrily, she opens her book again, and I know this conversation is over. Once again, I failed. I have no idea how to charm her or get her on my side again. But I am happy that she trusts Titus, even if the trust is a little misguided. He is a good man, unlike me.

The Retribution Kings made their greatest decision ever when they elected Titus as their new leader. He doesn't take enemies lightly. He won't start wars without a purpose. He'll find a way to make the initiation rules a thing of the past. He'll find a way to end the trauma and pain that comes with being a Retribution King. And with Lilith by his side, he'll accomplish his goals that much faster.

My thoughts swirl through my mind for the rest of the short flight from our home in Chicago. My eyes cut glances at Lilith, but I don't open my mouth to speak again. I'd have better luck hacking into her phone or digging through her bag to look for clues as to what we're doing on this trip.

We land, and I practically have to sprint to keep up with Lilith. She takes off through the airport, still not speaking to me, treating me like a true bodyguard—an employee, not a friend.

I noticed she's gripping her phone rather tightly in her hand, looking down at it every few minutes as she walks hastily through the airport. She almost runs into a few people, not really paying attention to where she's going. I eye her suspiciously but don't ask. I hope she'll forget I'm even here whenever she receives the message or call she's waiting for.

After exiting the security, she weaves into a thick crowd, and I'm forced to stop. A second later, she's gone.

"Fuck," I say under my breath.

I scan the area quickly, realizing she most likely did this on purpose. She wasn't taken by someone. I slow my breathing and heart rate down as I look for any sign of her.

That's when I notice the bathroom sign. I know instinctually that's where she went. I push through the crowd and walk as fast as I can to the bathroom. I lean against it, cracking it just a little to hear inside.

Her voice has my heart stuttering in relief. She did just choose to ditch me, and she wasn't taken by some enemy.

But what I hear is like a stab to the heart.

"I love you and miss you already."

Titus—she's already saying the words 'I love you' to Titus. And the way she's saying the words with such sincerity—she's not acting, she's not playing him. It's how she truly feels.

I ease the door shut, not baring to listen to another word she says. It changes everything and doesn't at the same time. She found her soulmate, a man both as vicious and as kind as she is. They make a good match, and she was never going to be mine.

She steps out of the bathroom a few minutes later and eyes me immediately.

"We're entering a competition. The winner gets an audience with The Abyss. They get to work with him, to form an alliance with him," she says.

I raise my eyebrows. "And why do we want to form an alliance with The Abyss?"

"He took something from Titus, and we're going to force him to give it back."

My brows furrow in confusion. "Why isn't Titus here himself then?"

"Titus is needed with the Retribution Kings. He can't spend weeks here doing the competition without the Retribution Kings thinking he's unfit to be their leader."

She doesn't give me a chance to question her plan.

"The Abyss is unknown. No one knows who he is. He's so secretive that many don't even think he actually exists. And this competition might be the only way to find out and then get revenge for Titus."

I stare at her in awe. This isn't about her sisters or friend. This is about Titus. This is about her love for him and possibly some deal the two struck. She does this for him, and he gets revenge for her.

But what did The Abyss take from Titus? And what will this cost them?

CHAPTER 10

Lilith

"WELL, THIS IS SAFE," Hayes says, as we stand in the doorway of our motel room.

I roll my eyes at him. "It's perfectly safe."

It's as safe as any fancy hotel room. But I eye a single bed with a thin mattress and what looks like a scratchy comforter. I doubt it is as comfortable as a five-star hotel room.

I move to step through the doorway, but Hayes throws an arm out in front of me. "Let me search first. Wait here."

I fold my arms across my chest but stand still as he moves past me and sweeps the room. His hand rakes over the lamp in the corner of the room, the single artwork above the bed that I think is supposed to be a picture of New York City but is too terrible to know for sure. He checks the night-stand, the creaky bed, the light switches, and the desk, even pulling out the chair and sitting on it. His weight breaks one of the legs, causing me to snicker. But he continues his search anyway, checking the TV and every inch of bare wall.

I huff and shut the door behind me when he comes up

empty. "I think the only danger in this room is you. I'm not gonna die from a shitty chair."

He ignores me and heads to the bathroom to continue sweeping for danger. I hear him opening and closing cabinets, turning the faucet on, and pulling the shower curtain back. He's clearly paranoid. I don't know what he expects to find in this motel room. *Cameras? A man who works for The Abyss hiding behind the shower curtain, ready to jump out and kill us?*

I fall back onto the bed, and the mattress bounces hard once, twice. I wince as the creak in the bed echoes through the room. Soon, the muffled noise of a TV next door fills our room through the paper-thin walls.

We aren't going to get much sleep here, but maybe that's part of the competition. It's supposed to mess with our psyche and ensure we don't get a good night's sleep. When the competition starts, The Abyss can test how well we perform sleep-deprived.

I yawn and close my eyes, exhausted from today. *Why does my life have to be so exhausting?*

I hear the floor shift as Hayes reenters the bedroom, but I don't open my eyes. I shouldn't trust him like this. I've threatened to kill him enough times that it would be smart of him to kill me before I kill him. But I know he won't. I know it more than I know that when I take another breath of air, it will fill my lungs and keep me alive. He doesn't want to kill me, not really. I trust that, at least.

"Tell me about these games," he says.

"What do you wanna know?"

"Are you the only one entering? Or both of us? Is it to the death? Don't you think we can find a better way to get a meeting with The Abyss than to enter a stupid competition? Even if we do win, we're putting a huge target on our back.

Others will know we have aligned with The Abyss," he rambles.

I sit up and open my eyes to stare at him. "The Retribution Kings have tried for years to figure out who The Abyss is. All efforts have failed. So no, I don't think there's another way. And yes, the games are to the death. There will only be one winner."

Hayes stills. "To the death?"

"That's what I said."

He shakes his head. "Are you insane?" His voice rises with every word.

I frown. For a split second, I want to throw one of my daggers into his neck to shut him up. I need him to stop doubting me.

"No, I'm not insane." I stand so that I'm face-to-face with him.

"You are insane if you're going to enter a competition to the death with a bunch of other men who spent their whole lives training to be as deadly as possible. You don't stand a chance—even you, murderous one."

"Oh, I'll win. I'll kill them all."

He takes a step towards me. "You won't. You're skilled but still young, naïve, and untested in many ways. You've just begun your training, even though you're already more skilled than almost anyone I've ever come across. You have a natural talent with knives and skills that will help keep you alive for a long time.

"But you're not ready yet. You don't have the experience of being attacked again and again by men double your size. You haven't been tricked and threatened and manipulated by the most evil men that walk this earth. And even if you could win, it's not worth it. Having a meeting with The Abyss isn't worth risking your life. I don't think they had anything to do with your sister's deaths. And even if they did, this isn't the way to get revenge. Winning this game won't bring them back."

White-hot anger floods through me. He doesn't think I can do this. There's a part of my subconscious that knows he's right, but I hate that he's calling me out on it. Of course, I won't enter a game like this on my own. I know I'm not skilled enough. I haven't finessed my skills enough. I don't have enough practice. And I know that if I'm the only woman in this game, I'm going to have a huge target on my back.

But it still infuriates me to hear him say it. He's just trying to piss me off enough to get me to divulge more information to him, but I'm not going to fall for it, not again.

"Titus believes in me, so why can't you? He's my husband. He loves me. And he doesn't think I'm going to die in these games. He thinks I'll win."

He shakes his head. "Then Titus is a fool. Maybe you can win, but it's not worth the risk. Your life is too important. It's way more important than the stupid mission he sent you on."

I throw one of my hidden knives at his dumb ass. My aim is perfect, nicking the outer tip of his right shoulder. A trickle of blood oozes through his white shirt and down his bicep.

Hayes's eyes swirl with dark amusement. He takes another step toward me, but I throw another two daggers at him. One hits his other shoulder; the other nicks his thigh.

"I don't know what's more impressive—your aim or the fact that you were able to get so many knives through airport security undetected."

My eyes narrow in response. "Don't underestimate me."
"Never," he agrees.

I only have one dagger left. I twirl it around in my hand, waiting for the right moment to win this argument. I watch him closely, looking for any sign of a weapon on his body. His jeans are tight, and I see no outline of a gun or knife, but I know one's there. He has to have a hidden weapon.

He moves with smooth determination—taking one step, then another, then another, until all I would have to do to kill him is jab my dagger up into his heart. It doesn't matter if he has a weapon on him or not—mine is out and ready. No matter how fast he moves, I can move faster. The only reason he's still breathing is because I desire it.

The air changes around us until I feel suffocated by it, suffocated by him.

I freeze.

He moves first.

Just jab—jab the dagger up against his chest and prove that I win, that I can win these games.

I glance down at his arms, waiting for them to grab a hidden weapon. But his hands drift up to my face.

I blink in confusion. My body tenses, readying my strike.

His fingers curl around my neck, his thumb brushing against my cheek. I melt against it for just a heartbeat before I realize what he's doing, but I'm too late.

His lips crash against mine in an engulfing kiss. It burns through my body, setting every nerve on fire. My mind goes blank. All I feel is him. His lips. His tongue sweeping into my mouth. His hardness pushing against my body until I'm limp in his arms.

His grip on my neck tightens, and then he's speaking against my lips. "You're dead," he says, pretending to snap my neck.

Fuck.

Fuck, fuck, fuck.

I shove him hard against the chest, realizing that I let my dagger go when he kissed me. I was defenseless. I let a stupid kiss get to me and unarm me.

He chuckles before his face turns serious again. "Those men will use every advantage they can. You will be a prime target, and they will play dirty to ensure you lose."

I smirk. "Good thing I didn't enter alone. It's a team game. I entered myself and Titus as a team."

Hayes frowns. "I thought you said Titus wasn't going to participate?"

"You'll pretend to be Titus. No one knows what Titus looks like since he's such a new leader. We will use that to our advantage."

CHAPTER 11

Hayes

"HERE'S YOUR COFFEE, my dearest wife," I say, handing her the paper cup filled with the dark sludge this motel calls coffee. I didn't dare travel to an actual coffee shop to get her coffee. It's too dangerous to leave her here alone, not when I don't really know the plan. I don't really know what she's after, and there are most likely countless dangerous men lurking throughout this motel.

She scowls at me but takes the cup. She sniffs the coffee, scrunching her nose up at the foul smell before taking a small sip. She frowns in disgust but takes another sip anyway.

"Don't call me that," she says.

"I haven't been around you long enough to know what Titus calls you. Does he call you baby? Wifey? Princess?"

"No," she says, getting out of bed and stomping toward the bathroom with her cup of coffee still in her hand.

I stalk after her, not letting her get away. She wants me to pretend to be her husband, then that's what she's going to get. I'll drive her mad until she tells me the truth of what we're doing here, or she gets rid of me.

She tries to slam the bathroom door in my face, but I slam my hand on it at the last second, stopping it from closing.

"Really? You aren't going to even let me pee in peace?"

I smile and tilt my head at her. "That wouldn't make me the doting husband, would it?"

She rolls her eyes at me. "Titus doesn't watch me pee."

"That's just because you're still in that honeymoon phase. And you've only stayed at places that are safe. This place is the opposite of safe, so I'm not taking my eyes off of you unless absolutely necessary."

She yawns, far too tired to fight me this early in the morning. Neither of us slept much last night. I pretended to sleep on the couch but mainly just replayed every word she spoke to me in my head, trying to figure her out. She didn't fare much better, even though she had the bed. The mattress is thin, and the box frame is noisy. Every time she rolled over it made a loud creaking sound, which was constant all night long.

She sets her cup of coffee on the counter and then pulls her shorts down to pee.

"So when and where does this competition start?"

"Sometime today, and I don't know where," she says grumpily.

I grin like a fool, loving when she gets all prickly and feisty like this. It does something to me, turns me on in a way that no other woman has turned me on before.

She pulls her pants up and flushes. "Stop looking at me like that. It's creepy."

"Looking at you like you're the hottest fucking woman in the world? Is that what you mean?"

She washes her hands. "Looking at me like you want to devour me. I'm not yours."

"I get to pretend you're mine for however long this competition lasts, *wife*."

"You don't have to pretend in his motel room now."

She turns toward me, ready to leave the bathroom, but my broad frame fills the doorway.

"I do, actually. You don't know who could be watching. The Abyss could have chosen this motel because they put cameras everywhere."

"Except you looked for cameras last night and found none. Try again."

"Just because I didn't find any doesn't mean they aren't here. And more importantly, we hate each other. It's clear as day to anyone watching us, too. We're supposed to be madly in love, a newly married couple. We need practice pretending we love each other."

"We don't need practice. And we have to just tolerate each other, not love each other. Everyone knows mafia bosses don't marry for love. They all assume it's an arranged marriage."

"You're not that good of an actress, grumpy. And you'll be better protected if they think we love each other, that it's not just an arrangement. No one wants to mess with the ruthless Retribution King, who is deeply in love with his wife and will kill anybody who dares to harm her. The loving act would offer you far more protection than them thinking you're just my pet, who I could easily replace with any other woman."

She shakes her head. "I don't need protection."

"Lies—that's why I'm here, to protect you."

She shoves me hard and then rushes past me. She turns her head back toward me.

"No, you're here because you owe me a debt. You killed my father. You will do whatever I say whenever I say it. And unfortunately, this is a man's world. So I can't enter this competition without a man by my side, a man that everyone thinks is in charge. You will pretend to be that man, but don't think for a second that you are in charge—I am. Or the next time I throw a dagger in your direction I won't miss your heart."

My lips curl up in a devious smile. "I love it when you threaten my life, vicious one."

She shakes her head in frustration and then stalks over to her bag. She pulls something small out and then turns to me, shoving it into my hand. "Here—this will go a long way to convincing people we're married."

I look down at the ring she's shoved into my hand.

"It's a replica of Titus's ring. He needed to keep his on to keep up appearances back home, but you need a ring here."

"You aren't going to slip it on my finger, wife?" I tease.

"If I did, I'd shove it on there so hard that it'd never come off again. I'd let it drain all the blood from your finger."

I laugh and slip the ring on. It feels strange on my finger. "I don't think a ring is going to do much to convince people of anything."

"People believe what you present to them. You, of all people, know that. It's why you're so good at getting women to spill their secrets. You throw them a smile, listen to them when they talk, pretend to be falling for them, and they believe you. This is no different. Present yourself as the arrogant, ruthless Retribution King with a pretty wife on your arm, and everyone will believe you. You're a good liar and actor, Hayes. I have no doubt that you'll do enough acting for the both of us to be believable."

"I'm not that good of an actor, Lily."

She stills. "Don't call me that."

"Lily? Why? Is that what Titus calls you?"

She doesn't answer me. She won't meet my gaze.

"I'm a dead man either way. Why should I put on a show?"

"Because you don't want me to die. You're too curious; you want to find out why I want to talk to The Abyss so badly."

I narrow my gaze at her, my eyes darkening. "Or I could just force you to tell me the truth."

"Good luck with that." She smirks. "I could force you, too. I know I'm not the only one keeping secrets."

We stare at each other. So much emotion. So much heartbreak. So much we can't or won't share with each other. And yet, when I look at her and she looks at me, we are the only people in the world for a split second. All I want to do is punish her with my kisses, fuck her until she's wrecked, and then tell her over and over again that I wish she were mine.

Her phone buzzes on the nightstand. She walks over and picks it up, reading the message out loud. "8 pm at Carbone restaurant."

She stares at me, waiting for my response. "Don't worry, Lily. I'll be there as your doting husband. I'll pretend for you. I'd even take a bullet for you. Together, we'll win. But don't blame me when after we win, your happy marriage falls apart. Because I don't plan on playing fair. You thought you fell in love with me before? Just wait."

CHAPTER 12

Lilith

JUST WAIT...

Those fucking words—they dominate my head making it impossible to think about anything else.

Just wait—a promise, a threat, and a hope.

You thought you fell in love with me before? Just wait.

Those words are going to haunt me, over and over and over, until I'm finally rid of Hayes.

Lily.

Why did I have to react when he called me Lily? Now that's all he'll call me. And every time he does, my heart is going to start fluttering, my breath will grow heavy, and warmth will caress my skin.

I don't hate him calling me Lily because that's Titus's nickname for me. I hate it because it's *Hayes's* nickname for me. It makes me think of before, when I thought Hayes loved me. Back when I thought it was all real, not some elaborate game we were playing with each other.

Hayes thinks he can get me to fall in love with him again. He thinks he's that charming, that lovable. He's that good at what he does that he can make me fall for him after every-thing he's done, even though I know he's faking it.

Gripping the sink with white knuckles, I stare at my reflection in the cracked mirror of the motel bathroom.

You will not fall for him, I tell myself. *He's a monster. He killed your father. He tricked you before. He's only looking out for his own interests.*

Butterflies swarm in my stomach, not from the impending beginning of the game we need to leave for in the next five minutes, but because of Hayes. I know he's pretending this time just to fuck with me, to try to keep me from killing him in the end, and yet, my heart still aches for him—yearns for something that was never real.

My cheeks flush, and my body tingles with anticipation as I ready myself to open the bathroom door. His reaction to just seeing me is going to weaken my knees. It's going to take everything in me to not let him rip my dress off me and let him fuck me on the creaky, flimsy bed.

I move to the door but stop myself. I breathe deeply and cool my emotions, trying to convince myself that I don't care about anything Hayes does. I can be a vicious monster, too. I can let whatever he says roll right off of me.

I'm married to Titus. Titus is my future, not Hayes. I'm the wife of the Retribution King leader. I'm powerful beyond imagination. And when I win this game, I'll have everything I could ever want.

When I open the door and walk out, head held high, I find Hayes sitting on the edge of the bed. He immediately stands as I enter the room, but I don't let my gaze hover on him. I barely let my eyes cut to him for a split second, just long enough to see he's in a blue suit, his long hair is pulled back, and glasses frame his green eyes. I don't let myself see his reaction.

"Let's go," I say, walking toward the door.

"Holy shit, Lily. I—uh—I..." Hayes stutters from behind me.

My hand stills on the doorknob as my heart thumps along with every syllable he breathes. I swallow down the lump in my throat before speaking.

"We don't have time for your theatrics. Let's go."

"Fuck," he curses under his breath.

He's good—so fucking good. But I'm better.

"Cut the crap, Hayes. I need you on top of your game tonight."

"Yes, Lily." His words are a caress against my bare neck. My hair is pulled on top of my head in red ringlets. My black dress is low cut everywhere, exposing more skin than I thought a dress could possibly reveal.

Somehow, Hayes moved so quickly and silently that I didn't realize he was right behind me until I felt his hot breath against my neck. Goosebumps dance down my arms and back. I try to turn the doorknob, but my fingers no longer work.

His hand moves over mine, turning my hand over the doorknob to open the door. He presses his body against mine, and I can feel how hard he is. He's so in control of his emotions and body to make me think he wants me—truly wants me—even though he hates me.

Neither of us moves as heat travels through my body.

I blink.

No, he's not going to win. I elbow him hard in the throat.

He gasps and then lets out a strangled chuckle as I push through the door and into the fresh, cool night air. The blast of chill prevents me from getting lost in his sexy trap again.

We don't speak as I drive us to the restaurant. Hayes offered, but I snapped at him. I needed the distraction that driving offers to keep from doing something stupid with

Hayes, like licking his rough jawline or tasting the corner of his lips.

I park the car in front of the valet, and we both get out. As I round the car, Hayes holds out his hand to me.

I scoff.

"The acting starts now. If you want to win, then play our roles. Luckily, your reaction earlier tells me it shouldn't be hard for you to have bedroom eyes and think about fucking me all night," Hayes says, pulling my arm through his.

"I did not have bedroom eyes," I say through clenched teeth.

He chuckles, "You did."

God, I'm going to kill him by the end of this just for his insufferable arrogance.

"Name?" a man in a black suit approaches us before we even enter the restaurant.

"Titus, leader of the Retribution Kings. And this is my wife, Lilith," Hayes says.

My wife—a thrilling chill races over my skin when he says the words.

This isn't real. I'm married to Titus. Titus is kind, and caring, and sweet. Hayes is a murderous liar.

"Follow me," the man says.

Hayes's eyes cut to me in a silent beg. This is my last chance to back out. Once we step foot through those doors, there is no escaping. We are entering the game to find out who The Abyss is, and we might die in the process.

I nod subtly to Hayes. I'm not backing out. This is too important.

Hayes sighs but continues to escort me into the building. We are taken to a private elevator and then up to the top floor of the building.

"Enjoy your dinner," the man says as we step out of the

elevator. Without giving us further instructions, the man takes the elevator back downstairs.

Hayes and I once again exchange glances, but then I take a step forward, and he matches me step for step.

"You look beautiful, by the way. You always look beautiful. But I know you didn't choose that dress for me. You don't want me to ogle you or notice you at all. You wore it as a distraction for the men here, so they won't think of you as a threat." He whispers the words against the shell of my ear.

"You may do an effective job of making yourself not seem like a threat, but you just made my job so much harder. Every man is going to want to fuck you. And I'll kill every man who tries."

"No man is going to want to..." I still, as a hush falls over the room, and I feel dozens of eyes on me. I don't know how to react as I scan the room. I thought I was prepared for this. I'm used to men staring. And after what I went through when the Retribution Kings were bidding on me, I should definitely be used to it.

But the intensity with which the men are looking at me —like Hayes brought dessert for them all to enjoy—makes my skin crawl.

Hayes pulls me against his side, and his head dips low until his mouth hovers over my ear. "I won't let them touch you. You're safe."

Then he runs his tongue over the shell of my ear. I blush as shivers work their way down my body.

Hayes slides my hand down his arm and interlocks our fingers. I didn't realize how much I needed the reassurance until his hand squeezed mine.

I roll my shoulders back and force myself to remain calm as we enter the private dining room.

"You brought your pet with you. I assume you're planning on sharing her to get some allies?" a man says from our right. In his black dress pants and shirt, his wild eyes and short, cropped black hair unease me.

Hayes stops, snapping his head in the man's direction. "I brought *my wife*. She's the only ally I need."

The man snorts. "Her? She looks more like a whore than a wife. She's far too scrawny to do anything except slow you down."

"Don't react," Hayes whispers into my ear. He knows I'm itching to grab one of my knives and kill this man.

"Speak that way about my wife again, and it will be the last thing you do," Hayes growls.

The man chuckles, throwing his head back. "You must be the new Retribution King leader. I heard he recently took a wife. I didn't realize you fell in love with the first whore who would open her legs for you."

The room bursts into fits of laughter.

Hayes moves as if to punch the man, but we can't risk that. We could be thrown out of the competition or make countless enemies, all because someone called me a whore. I know Hayes is sensitive to the word, but he can't react.

"Don't react," I whisper to him, keeping my lips as still as possible, repeating his words back to him.

"I am Titus, leader of the Retribution Kings, and this is my wife, Lilith. And you can say whatever you want about our relationship. Call me a fool for falling in love, when we all know love is a weakness in this world. But my love for Lilith is my greatest strength. You'll see that soon enough," Hayes responds.

I gape at his words and then snap my mouth shut, forcing all emotion from my face. Hayes is pretending to be Titus. He's pretending. None of the words he speaks are true.

He squeezes my hand again as we walk through the room, studying all of the men but not approaching any of them. We need space after that conversation. At least no more laughter follows us after Hayes's speech.

We're offered alcohol by the wait staff, but we both refuse. We need all of our strength and wit to win this game.

"Do you know any of the men here?" I ask.

Hayes shakes his head. "No."

It puts us at a disadvantage as it seems many of the other men know each other. They may already have alliances, while we have none. But still, neither of us make a move to make nice with the others or learn anything about them.

"Who do you think is in charge?" I ask, not able to make out who has been tasked by The Abyss to run this competition. There doesn't seem to be anyone organizing the group.

Hayes scans, his eyes narrowing. "I don't see anyone in charge."

Waiters bring out the first course, and everyone gravitates toward the single long table. We find two seats together toward the end of the table, hoping to avoid the stares of the others and be in a position to make a quick escape if we need to.

There's an uneasy tension in the room as we all eat course after course. The others converse with each other, but Hayes and I keep our conversation limited and only talk to each other, careful not to reveal anything to those sitting near us.

As dessert is brought out, I feel a searing stare from the man across the long table from us. He watches me intently, as I lift my spoon filled with chocolate decadence to my mouth.

"Do you truly think you can keep her alive and still win?" the man says, looking from me to Hayes.

"Yes," Hayes says simply and firmly.

"That's stupid. It's already foolish enough for you to

enter yourself instead of sending your men to risk their lives for you," the man replies.

"I don't send my men to risk their lives if I'm not willing to risk it myself. You're the same," Hayes says, guessing that the man is a leader.

The man smiles grimly. "Seth Marsh, leader of The Shadows."

Hayes nods. "I guess I'm not the only fool here."

The man shakes his head, looking from Hayes to me. "I wasn't foolish enough to fall in love or bring that love into a vicious competition that will kill her."

I bite my tongue, knowing it's best not to let anyone here know how skilled I am until the last possible moment. But it's becoming harder and harder for me to keep my mouth shut.

"Lilith won't die—that's a promise I intend to keep," Hayes said.

"The rules were clear. There will only be one winner. Everyone else dies. Only one gets to meet The Abyss."

"And that will be Lilith."

The man looks to me, like he knows he's tried his best with Hayes and isn't getting anywhere. "He can't protect you. No one can. I suggest you leave now before the competition starts and you have no choice but to continue. And if you want real advice, you'll find a new husband, one who won't lead you into peril because of his own ego."

I snap.

I don't know if this man is just genuinely trying to help me or stir shit up. But either way, he's not having this conversation with anyone else here. He's only saying this because I'm a woman, and he thinks I'm weak.

I open my mouth, but before a syllable leaves my lips, Hayes's lips crash onto mine. His hand wraps around the back of my neck, sealing our lips together. My eyes squeeze shut as his tongue slips between the seam of my lips, finding my tongue.

I'm so shocked that the only thing I can do is kiss him back. I can only enjoy this fleeting moment. I'll never get to experience it again after this competition is over.

I should feel guilty for kissing a man who isn't my husband. Even though this is pretend, and even though Hayes just kissed me to keep me from saying something that would have revealed my true skillset, I should feel guilty.

But I grip the fabric of his shirt, holding him to me, begging the kiss to keep going. It's the only drop of pleasure I might feel for the rest of my short life. While I have every intention of winning, there are no guarantees. Hayes can't promise that I'll live any more than I can promise that he'll live. Even if we win these games, we are destined to die young.

A high-pitched whistle rings out, and we break apart. Hayes's hooded eyes stare at me as he breathes hard. If this were real, I'd say his eyes are holding a promise of what he plans to do to me the second we are alone. But I know now that it's all part of his own personal twisted game. It's an act he's perfected with women to give him all the power.

Seth is scowling at us, and we have caught the attention of every man. They are either whistling, frowning, or smirking at us. Some are making snide remarks. Hayes just made things worse instead of better for us, and now we have a huge target on our backs.

Suddenly, everyone's phones start vibrating. I pull my phone out of the clutch I'm carrying and hold it out for Hayes to read along with me.

"I have hidden expensive jewels on half the competitors. The other half have none. In three days' time, whoever has a jewel will continue in the competition. And whoever doesn't will be eliminated. The competition starts now."

CHAPTER 13

Hayes

"DON'T REVEAL anything until we get out of here," I say under my breath.

She nods, her eyes scanning the room as everyone finishes reading the text and starts searching for the jewels on them. Only a handful are smart enough to not search so publicly.

"We need to go," I whisper.

"One second," she says, still scanning the men.

I quickly make my own assessment, but my main priority is getting us out of here before all hell breaks loose. I'm not going to let her die here.

I grab her hand, yanking her out of her chair and pulling her toward the exit. Her eyes stay on the others in the room, making assessments until the last second when I push her through the exit door.

"Run," I yell at her as I push her into the stairwell, immediately realizing my mistake as we have over a dozen flights of stairs to climb down to get out of this building. But we didn't have a choice. The elevator is a death trap in a situation like this.

We make it down one flight of stairs before we hear footsteps thundering down behind us.

"Fucking heels," Lilith curses, kicking them off.

My eyes widen. *How could I have been so stupid to let her wear heels without bringing a change of shoes?*

We don't have time for thoughts of that or of thoughts of that kiss.

It was a mistake—the kiss. It was also incredible and left me thinking I was an idiot for ever betraying her. For letting Titus have her. For not finding a way to keep her.

My mind can't think about that. I put all my focus into moving one leg in front of the other as fast as I can down the stairs, keeping up with Lilith, while hoping that Lilith can move faster.

Lilith's hair begins to fall with each step down the stairs and sweat glistens on the back of her neck. Suddenly, Lilith jolts to a stop as she turns the corner to go down another set of stairs.

"Fuck," she curses, looking to where her dress is caught on the handrail.

I grab the black fabric and rip it quickly before practically shoving her down the stairs as I hear the footsteps behind us closing in.

"Faster!" I bark.

She forces her legs faster. I match her steps, making sure my body is shielding hers with every step. I'm not sure until we make it to the bottom door if we are going to make it or not.

She flings the door open, and we both go barreling out. She tries to stop to catch her breath, but I don't let her. I'd carry her if I thought it would make us go faster or keep her safer, but I have to keep my body between her and the men.

"Keep running!"

She does, not questioning me for a second. I know her

feet must ache from running on the pavement, but she can't stop. We can't stop.

"Right!" I yell at her, seeing a small alleyway where we might be able to catch our breath for a second.

She dashes right, and I slide into the thin alleyway no wider than my shoulders. It's more of a gap than an alleyway, but this is better. She's completely protected by my body.

"It's a little wider back here," she says.

I follow her voice in the darkness and find that the gap doubles in width, but we are at a dead end. We can't stay here long, but it's the best place to catch our breaths and come up with a plan.

"Do you have a jewel?" she asks with hope in her voice.

I begin searching my pockets, my jacket, my shoes, and every inch of fabric for any small jewel. Lilith watches me closely.

"I don't think so," I say, my voice dropping. It would be far easier to keep a jewel for three days than to have to take one from someone else.

"Are you sure?" she asks, her voice trembling slightly.

"You're free to look."

That's all the invitation she needs, and her hands are on my body. First, my jacket pockets, then skimming the buttons on my shirt, and then my pants pockets. Her touch is mechanical and efficient, but my body reacts to her touch nonetheless. My breathing halts, and my heart beats rapidly as her hands accidentally brush against my length.

"I don't think anyone hid a jewel there without me noticing, Lily."

She swallows hard. "Sorry."

"I assume since you are searching me so thoroughly, it means that you haven't found a jewel on you."

She sighs. "No, but look for me, please. Maybe I missed something."

My throat bobs. There aren't many places to hide a jewel on her body. There are no pockets on her dress.

I take her clutch, searching it thoroughly before I take my phone out and shine the light up and down her body. Her black dress turns sheer under the light, and I can make out far too much of her body. But there is no shimmer of a jewel reflecting back at me.

I pocket my phone before walking toward her, my eyes stilling on hers. Her soft gaze is the only permission I get. I place my hands in her hair that has fallen out of the updo she had on top of her head. I gently pull the curls down as I dig my fingers in her hair; her eyes close as I tug, hoping a jewel will fall free.

My fingers skim her neck and over the swell of her breasts. Her nipples harden under my touch when I realize she isn't wearing a bra.

"Sorry," I say.

"No, you're not," she breathes.

I chuckle. "You're right; I'll take any chance I can to touch you."

My hands continue down her slim waist and then over her hips, feeling nothing but the smooth fabric of her dress. When I get to the slit in her dress, I let my hands go underneath the fabric, feeling her toned thigh as I kneel in front of her.

I grin up her, trying to break the tension as I let my hands rise—finding her gun and blade strapped to her thighs.

"Such a dangerous thing," I mutter, staring into the spot between her thighs.

When my hands skim over her panties, she grabs my hands and stops my teasing.

"There are no jewels there."

I smirk. "I disagree."

She rolls her eyes as I rise.

"We don't have a jewel," Lilith says.

I sigh. "It doesn't appear so."

She runs her hand through her hair. "Fuck."

I agree but don't say anything.

"What do we do?" I ask, knowing she already has a plan forming beneath that mop of red hair I want to tangle my hands in. While I was busy ensuring that she stayed alive, she was assessing. She chose a target already. She knows which of the men most likely have a jewel and which don't.

"You're not going to like it." She bites her lip as she paces.

Clearly, she doesn't like her plan that much, either.

"Spit it out."

She stops pacing. "We use me as bait."

"What? How is that a plan? We can't use you as bait when we don't have a jewel."

"Really? You know that's not true. Every man there either wanted to fuck me to show me how much of a man they are, or they wanted to be the one to kill me."

I frown, hating it.

"They all saw how quickly we ran. Everyone will assume that means we have a jewel."

She's right, and I hate it.

"No," I say grumpily.

"Do you have a better idea?"

Now I'm pacing—two feet left and then two feet to the right. That's all I can move in this small space.

"There has to be a better plan than letting one of those men capture you," I say.

"There isn't. It's the best plan, especially since we don't

want them to know how skilled I am until we have to. It could mean the difference between winning and losing."

I know she's right, but I refuse to admit that out loud.

"Who should be our target?"

"Reginald, he works for the The Void. He's not the weakest here, so he won't be everyone's main target. But he's not the strongest either. And the way he was looking at me all night tells me he'll fall for the bait. He wants me. And I saw the outline of a jewel in his front pocket."

"He wants to murder you or fuck you?" I ask, each word burning in my throat.

"Both."

I shiver. *Fuck this fucking plan.*

"Use me as bait instead."

"You know that won't work. You have to be the one free to save me."

I still. "You trust me to save you once you're captured?"

"Yes."

I shake my head, but I can't come up with any other way either. Her plan will work. She's strong enough to save herself if she has to, but I care about her too much to not save her first.

CHAPTER 14
Lilith

I SPOT Reginald exactly where I knew he would be: his safe space. It's also the only place he's known to visit every night—a strip club.

He's sitting in a booth, getting a lap dance while two bodyguards sit on either side of him.

Too fucking easy.

I scan the club, looking for any of the other competitors. I can't be the only one who saw that Reginald had a jewel and figured out where he would spend his days. But on a quick scan, I don't see anyone familiar. That doesn't mean they aren't here, but only that I can't see them.

I look around for Hayes, but I don't see him either. I don't expect to see him necessarily, but I know he's here. If he can't be by my side, then I at least wish he was in my ear —telling me what he sees.

But we didn't have enough time to get the gear to stealthily communicate with each other. We are both doing this on blind trust.

The probing stage lights blind me every few seconds as I

walk toward Reginald. My hands clam up, and my legs tremble slightly. I only have one hidden knife on me—one.

It's the only protection I have if Hayes fails to get to me in time. If Reginald searched me and found all of my weapons on me, then he'd realize I'm more skilled than I've let on. That surprise might save my life, so I need to keep it hidden for now.

I fluff my loose red curls, rub my lips together with a new coat of lipstick, and strut as hard as I can in my swanky black dress with the slit cut even higher. I'm sure the second Reginald sees me he'll know who I am, but it doesn't matter. All that matters is that he lets me get close to him.

I stop right in front of his booth, and his bodyguards don't even twitch a muscle. They don't see me as a threat at all.

Good.

But Reginald sees me. His eyes cut to me and off the blonde on his lap.

"Want to play with me instead?" I purr, my voice as sultry as I can make it. I lick my lips for good measure, but Reginald isn't looking at my lips. His intense stare falls on my breasts.

I don't move. I let him look, let my body do the talking.

Reginald snaps his fingers, and the bodyguard to his left takes the blonde by the hand and leads her off.

I smile smugly—*too easy.*

I start walking toward him, ready to take her place and give him one hell of a lap dance.

"Not here," he says. Then I feel them. I don't know how many, but there are men completely surrounding me.

My heart jumps in my throat. Even if I had all my weapons, I'm not sure I could take down this many men by myself. I'm not sure if Hayes can even handle this many.

I try not to think about that as they escort me to a back

room. One of them grabs me by the bicep, leading me. I want to bite his fingers off, but I don't react. I let them think this is exactly what I want.

Once inside the back room, I see how outnumbered we really are—a dozen.

Fuck. I'm so totally fucked.

Reginald enters the room last, looking pleased.

"I knew someone would come. That's why I didn't run. I hid out in the place I know best. This is my castle. I just didn't think you would be dumb enough to come alone, princess."

I scowl. "Don't call me that."

"Search her."

The second the order leaves his lips, three men surround me and grope me, searching for a weapon.

I let them while I stare down Reginald. His murky grey eyes and scarred skin don't scare me, and neither do the touches of his men.

"She's clean, sir," one of the men says.

They didn't find my single blade tucked tightly against my ribcage where the fabric of my dress is thickest.

Reginald nods and walks toward me, his eyes searching me head to toe.

"What's strange is Titus sending you here. Why would he do that? A distraction, perhaps? Or does he not love you like he claimed? Are you dispensable? Just a pawn he can use to deceive the rest of us?"

"Touch me and find out," I snark.

He smiles, walking around me as if by just looking at me, he can discover what I am to Titus. He stops in front of me, becoming eye to eye with me.

"I don't have the jewel on me, princess. How foolish of me would it be to make myself an easy target and then keep the jewel here."

"If you don't have the jewel on you, it's only because someone got to you first before I did. It's certainly not because you were smart enough to hide it somewhere else."

He smirks. "So feisty. I can see why Titus fell for you. I'm going to enjoy breaking you piece by piece until your lover gets here. Don't worry, I won't play with you too hard until then. He deserves to get to watch you die with his own eyes."

I growl, snapping at his taunt.

But before I take more than a step toward Reginald, men on either side of me grab my arms and yank them back. Instead of slipping out of their grasp, I put up a weak and defenseless struggle.

Reginald's lip curls up in satisfaction as zip-ties bind my wrists together behind my back, and a soft fabric is shoved into my mouth and tied behind the back of my head to keep me from talking.

"That's better. Now we don't have to listen to you talk while we wait for your Retribution King to come and get his...retribution. That is, if he even truly cares about you enough to get revenge for you. But he certainly won't be able to save your life."

Reginald turns away from me, but I see his movement. I see his hand slip inside his right jacket pocket. He was checking to see if I had taken the jewel. His shoulders relax the second he realizes it's still there.

I twitch, but otherwise, don't react. He has the jewel on him. I was right. Now, all I can do is wait for Hayes. He'll come; I know he will. *But will it be soon enough?*

CHAPTER 15

Hayes

"DON'T FUCKING FOLLOW HIM," I curse under my breath. But of course, she can't hear me, and of course, she follows him into the back room. I'm not sure she'd listen to me even if she could hear me.

She's the most stubborn, determined, self-sufficient, unafraid person I've ever met. And this mission she agreed to do for Titus—whatever it actually is—has become the most important thing in the world to her. It's beyond just needing to stay alive to win the game. Even if we somehow survived the game but lost, it would devastate her.

I sigh, not allowing myself a second to worry about her. She's counting on me to help her. If she reveals that she can fight her way out, we'll become an even bigger target. Right now, everyone is just amused by me bringing a woman into this. They don't yet see us as a threat. But once she reveals she's as skilled or more so than they are, they'll hunt her to the ends of the earth.

So for now, she has to rely on me to save her.

I scan the club, counting how many of his men I can

make out. There are at least two dozen. No wonder Reginald came here. He felt safe here. His men are here.

And then I look to the servers—all women. *Do they work for him? Do they know the type of man they work for?*

I consider my options, but there aren't many.

My heart clenches as I stare down at my watch. I have five minutes. I'm not going to leave Lilith alone with that man for more than five minutes.

I take a step to my left as the brown-haired woman with a haunted look in her eyes passes me. Our shoulders knock together.

"I'm so sorry," I say, a grin curling up on my lips as I take her in, pretending she's the most beautiful woman I've ever seen in my life.

She blushes at my reaction. "It's okay."

"Hayes, my name is Hayes." I take her hand so she won't run away and kiss the back of it.

She freezes, and her cheeks darken.

"I don't usually do this, but you're so beautiful, and I feel this instant connection between us."

She shakes her head. "You don't think I've heard that line every night I've worked here?"

I'm sure she has, but never from someone as good-looking as me. Never from someone her age. Never from someone she actually wants to hit on her.

I move my body closer, guessing I only have three minutes left on my self-determined time limit.

"I'm sorry, I just..." I don't have time to waste. I pull her to me until her body is flush against mine, and I kiss her. She tastes like cherry lip balm and cigarettes. She's far too tall and doesn't fit into my body correctly.

She gasps against my lips but doesn't pull away or push me away.

I let my lips linger on her, my eyes stay closed for a

second longer than necessary as I pretend to savor the kiss like it was the best damn kiss of my life. When I finally open my eyes and look down at her, she's staring at me like I just saved her life.

I run my thumb across her lip. "That was..." I say, feigning speechlessness.

She bites her bottom lip.

"When do you get off work?" I ask, breathless.

"Not until two a.m.," she says in frustration.

"I can't wait that long." I run my hand through her hair, tucking a strand behind her ear.

She shivers at my touch. "Me neither."

"I saw a back room that looks vacant." I point to the door that Lilith entered with Reginald and his men.

She grins like I just had the best idea in the world. She pulls out a card from her pocket and slides it into my palm. "You'll need this."

"What about security cameras? I don't want to get you in trouble with your boss." My words drip with hot need.

She gulps. "There's a breaker box at the end of the hallway just past that door. Kill the power, and the security cameras won't work."

"Thank you, Jamie," I say, reading her name tag. I squeeze her hand and give her one last seductive grin. I'm pretty sure the cameras will still work even if I kill the power, but that doesn't matter. What does matter is that I can kill the power to the room.

"I'll meet you there as soon as I go on break in about an hour."

I run my tongue across my bottom lip and release her. "Can't wait."

Jamie stumbles away. I keep my eyes on her until she turns away from me. Then I glance down at my watch—six minutes.

Fuck.

I move swiftly but not as fast as I want. I don't want to draw attention to myself. I couldn't have picked a better target than Jamie. For a second, I almost feel guilty for preying on her, but then I remember that Lilith is probably seconds away from getting violated or killed.

After using Jamie's keycard to get into the hallway, I kill the power and run to the back room, drawing my gun.

I fire a silenced shot at the man guarding the door, and he falls with a thud to the ground.

One down, eleven to go.

I make swift work of the next three. But I don't know where Lilith is. The darkness hides everything from me unless they are within ten feet of me. It's both an advantage and a disadvantage. They don't know how many people are attacking them, which causes chaos. But if I don't move fast enough, they'll kill Lilith before I get to her.

I feel my heart beating in my throat. She's going to be fine. I made it to her in time. She's going to be fine, I repeat over and over, not accepting anything else.

I focus on the task: shooting or slicing into any man before they even get a bullet off in my direction.

I've only taken down half the men when I raise my gun again, ready to squeeze the trigger, and I see a wisp of red curl fly in front of my face.

"Lilith," I breathe.

She spins, facing me with a grin on her face. "You're late," she teases.

I scan the room, not feeling anyone else's presence. "And you took down six men with a single blade."

She shrugs like it was nothing.

It wasn't nothing. It is everything.

I grab her wrists and yank her to me, kissing her desperately. I'm sure she'll pull away, but she doesn't.

Her tongue thrusts into my mouth like she's punishing me for showing up late. She had the same internal clock ticking down, and she knows I was two minutes later than I planned.

"I'm sorry," I purr against her lips, kissing her again as I tangle my hand in her hair. I don't let her go; I hold her flush against my body. Feeling every inch of her soft, warm flesh as it melts against me. And I know she feels it, how much I want her. This isn't just a game to me, either.

But she says nothing when I finally release her.

"What was that for?" she huffs.

With fire in my eyes, I say, "You're my wife, and I almost lost you. I'm never going through that again."

She shakes her head but doesn't say anything, keeping the ruse up in case there are cameras.

"Was it worth it?" I ask.

She steps to Reginald's body, lying on the ground in a pool of his own blood. She stands over him, straddling her feet to avoid stepping in the blood. Bending down, she reaches into his jacket pocket and pulls out a small red jewel.

She smirks at me in that way only she can—a taunting grin.

"You tell me."

"How close was I from being too late?" I ask, my breath heavy.

She swallows, and there's a chill across her face before she speaks. "There is no such thing as being too late when you're willing to risk everything."

CHAPTER 16

Lilith

HAYES STARES at me without a hint of amusement on his face. It's so strange seeing him serious. Lately, he's been more serious than ever before. I expect him to crack a joke, to smile, to agree with me. Instead, his face turns into a blank shield of emotion as he watches me merely a few feet away.

I was fucked, I want to tell him. There was nothing I could do. I couldn't get out of the bindings. I couldn't fight off that many men. I had no plan to figure out how to escape. I was dead if he didn't show up when he did.

But I don't tell him that. This won't be the last time I have to risk my life in order to win this competition. And I need Hayes to trust me when I come up with plans. I need him to believe me when I say I can do it.

An easy smile spreads across his lips as he approaches me. His smile really is the most beautiful thing I've ever seen. It's mesmerizing and warm.

I smile back even though mine doesn't reach my eyes. *How could it, after what happened?*

"We should get out of here, and figure out a plan now that we have the jewel," I say.

He stops, grabbing my wrist and examining my skin. There's a thin red line at the seam of my wrists. He sweeps my hair from my neck and spots another red mark, where a trickle of blood is oozing from the shallow cut there.

His eyes race over my body frantically, looking for more marks, more places I was touched.

My heart races, and my tears well as I start thinking about what happened to me. About how close that knife came to slicing through an artery. About the tongue that grazed my cheek. About the hands that palmed my breasts and down the front of my body like I was his, while I was voiceless with a gag in my mouth.

Hayes stops his scanning, noticing my squirming. He takes my hand once again and kisses the tender spot on the inside of my wrist. Then he takes my other hand and does the same to the other wrist. His lips then brush against the mark on my neck.

I close my eyes, letting myself feel his touch.

"I'm sorry," he whispers as he kisses every drop of skin he can find—my cheeks, neck, arms, hands, and upper swell of my breasts. He marks my body with his lips, reminding me that I'm safe and that he cares about me. And it's almost as if he's marking me as his.

My eyes fly open, watching him closely.

I'm not his.

Hayes is just really good at what he does. He's good at pretending. He's good at manipulating women into getting what he wants.

Suddenly, I have another question.

"How did you get in here? How did you shut off the power?"

"I flirted with a woman who works here."

I frown.

"And I would have flirted and kissed a hundred women if it meant saving you."

He grabs my wrist and yanks me hard to him, capturing my lips with his own once again. This time, I don't yield. I slam my fist into his stomach, knocking the wind out of him. But before I can move, he's pulled me hard until my back is to his front, and that strong arm of his is wrapped around my chest.

He whispers in my ear, "Play nice, or else those watching on the cameras won't think we are husband and wife."

Anger boils in my chest, and I elbow him hard in the ribs, but he doesn't let go. I kick and flail in his arms, and still, he doesn't let me go.

"Stop fighting me," he growls.

"Never."

He chuckles. "Good, you're still in there. They didn't break you." And then he lets me go.

He goaded me into fighting, into letting go of the pain of what happened to me.

I glare at him.

He grins widely back. "I told you I was going to make you fall in love with me."

I growl. "I am not in love with you, and I never will be, you arrogant, manipulative bastard."

"And you're a lying, beautiful fighter."

I shake my head, not responding to him. "Let's go."

I'm fuming, but also, I know he just helped me. He helped me let go of the fear of what could have happened by being both sweet and an asshole.

I stop thinking about Hayes and his messed up motives as I lead us out the back of the club and into the darkness of the night.

"What now?" he asks.

I palm the jewel. We have the jewel, but after the body count and security footage we just left all over that club, it won't be hard for anyone to realize we have a jewel and to come after us.

Two days—we have to keep the jewel and stay alive for two days.

"How much cash do you have?" I ask.

"None."

"Fuck," I say, knowing we're going to leave a trace.

He chuckles. "You know who I am and the skills I have. We don't need cash."

I shoot a snarky look in his direction.

"Lilith Hart, are you jealous? Do you not want me to flirt with other women?"

"No, I don't. Those women deserve better."

"Uh-huh," he says, staring at me.

I glare at him.

"So, then, what's the plan?" He raises his eyebrows, waiting for me to answer.

I'm not wearing shoes; my dress is torn, and my hair is a tangled mess. I'm sure my makeup is running. We need a change of clothes and a good night's sleep to survive whatever tomorrow will bring.

I sigh. "Fine, you win. We'll do it your way."

CHAPTER 17

Lilith

HAYES DRAGS us to the swankiest hotel we can manage to walk to, our legs aching with exhaustion. It feels like we've walked all night, but we didn't dare stop anywhere close.

"I'm going to need my shoes back," Hayes says, staring down at my feet as we stand in the lobby.

I sigh but kick them off before bending down to fasten my heels back to my blistered feet.

Hayes puts on his shoes quickly and with ease. Meanwhile, I fight with the straps on my shoes and try not to wince too dramatically when they rub against my blisters.

"I can give you a piggyback ride if you want."

"And how would you hit on another woman with me on your back?"

His arrogant ass grins. "I have my ways."

I just shake my head, but I almost want to see it —almost.

"So what's your plan exactly?"

"You'll see," he replies.

I sigh, hating this. But we don't have a lot of options. We

need to leave as little a trace as possible for the others to find us.

Hayes leads the way, exploring the first floor of the fancy hotel he picked out. I stay close and scan for any signs of our competition or anything at all that would make us think twice about staying here.

The hotel lobby is brightly lit, and there is a small bar to the right of the entrance. It's crowded as everyone gets their last drinks before calling it a night.

I linger in the lobby as Hayes starts walking toward the bar.

He stops, turning toward me. "What are you doing?"

"I'm just going to wait here for you to do your thing."

He narrows his gaze as if he's looking through me. "You're coming with me."

I shake my head. "I'm perfectly safe here. No one can grab me without the police being called on them."

"Lily," he says, his voice dripping with a please.

My throat bobs. I'm not sure I can handle watching him flirt his way into the bedroom of another woman. And once he does, I'm not sure what his plan is. *Would he actually fuck her while I hide in the closet? Or would he tie her up some-where while we use her bedroom?* Either way, this won't end well, and I want to see as little as possible.

He takes my hand gently. "Trust me."

My hands are clammy in his, but I do trust him. I just don't trust him with my heart.

Still, I let him hold my hand. His fingers intertwine with mine in a firm grasp. He leads me toward the bar, never letting go of my hand.

I stride with him, trying my best to ignore the beautiful brunette he's walking toward at the bar. *I can't do this*, I think over and over. My hands grow cold, and my heart speeds in my chest.

He's not mine, I remind myself. *I chose another. Titus is mine, not Hayes. I have no claim over him beyond my hired bodyguard.*

But my heart doesn't listen. It thrums with nervous energy and sends adrenaline through my veins like fire. I suddenly have the urge to beat up any woman who even bats an eyelash at Hayes.

Somehow, despite everything we've been through, Hayes still looks hot. The buttons on the top of his shirt are undone, and sweat coats his brow, but he's managed to redo his man bun, and no one would guess he's anything but an honored guest at this hotel. On the other hand, I look completely disheveled, like I've been living on the street the past few days.

I squeeze my eyes shut, not wanting to see the look he's going to give this woman when we get to the bar. I wish I could block out the sound of his voice as well.

"Sit here, baby," he says, his voice dripping with a honey-sweet tone.

He helps me onto the chair next to the brunette I assume he's going to flirt with. *But maybe he's choosing the bartender or some other target? Or maybe he's just dropping me somewhere he thinks I'll be safe while he finds his target?*

But no, he sits down next to me, looking at me with deep concern in his eyes.

"Baby, I'm so sorry. I'm so fucking sorry." His hands grip the sides of my face as he says the words. Then his hands are everywhere—all over my hair, my cheeks, my neck—inspecting me as if he's going to find some horrible injury on me.

I frown, completely lost at what he's doing.

He gives me a subtle wink that does strange things to my heart, and then continues on.

"Are you okay? Where are you hurt?"

"I'm fine," I grumble.

"You're not fine. You were attacked, mugged, you could have..." his voice trembles and cracks.

I notice the woman behind me staring at me, her jaw slack in shock as she takes me in. I certainly look like I've been mugged.

"I'm sorry I failed you. I should have been there. I should have..." his face drops into my lap as a sob escapes his throat.

I stroke his head, not really sure what part he wants me to play. I savor the feeling of his strands of hair between my fingers again.

His head rises, tears stroking down his cheeks. "I'm sorry. I was just parking the car. I thought you'd be safe. This is a safe part of town. I'm so sorry, Lily."

He chokes back a sob. "I've loved you since the moment I laid eyes on you, since I saw you in that green dress. Ever since I kissed you under that willow tree, I knew I was yours. My heart belongs to you. I wish it had been me. I wish I was the one mugged and attacked, my life threatened—not you. It should have never been you."

Tears streak down his face again. "I don't know what I'd do if I lost you. You are the love of my life. You are my everything. I don't deserve you. I don't deserve you..."

"Shhh, it's okay. I'm okay," I say, but my own voice breaks.

His words eat at me, mixing the lines between truth and fiction. My heart aches to hear those words. I want nothing more for them to be true, but then I remember. He killed my father; he tricked me. This is what he does—he tricks women to get what he wants.

A second later, the woman next to me gets up from her chair and approaches us.

"I'm sorry, I overheard your conversation, and I just

need to say something. I'm so sorry what you went through, but you have to forgive him. He did nothing wrong. You won't find a better man than him in this city," she says.

I swallow hard. "I know."

"So, you'll forgive him?" the woman asks me, staring at me like she has a right to know that information.

"It's complicated," I answer.

The woman frowns, not liking my answer one bit. She turns to Hayes, who has sat back in his chair but is still gripping both of my hands tightly.

The woman leans in, giving him a hug. "You'll get through this. I hope she forgives you, but I don't think there is anything she needs to forgive you for."

Her voice drops, but I still make out her words. "And if she doesn't, here's my number."

She slides a card into the palm of his hand, and then she walks away. I have to force myself to stay seated in my chair instead of going after her and kicking her ass.

When I turn back to Hayes, he has the goofiest grin spread across his face.

"What was that about?" I snarl.

He chuckles. "That was me flirting with a woman to get us a hotel room."

"I didn't see her offer to get us a hotel room. I saw her giving you her number."

"She did," he says, chucking the card with her number on it onto the bar. "Which is why you won't feel guilty about spending her money."

"What do you—"

Hayes holds up her credit card.

My eyes widen. "When did you...? How did you...?"

He smiles, cocking his head to one side as he brushes a strand of my hair out of my face. "I said I'd flirt with a woman, but I didn't say which woman. You just so happen to be my favorite woman to flirt with."

I roll my eyes. "Those sobs and tears were for her, not for me."

"No, they were all for you."

"How did you get the card?"

"When she hugged me, I grabbed this out of her wallet."

I stare at it—our only hope of hiding tonight.

"If she reports it, others could track us here, realizing we used a stolen card."

He nods. "Yes, but I doubt she will report it in the next two days. She has so many cards in there; she won't miss this one."

I grin. "I don't think I'll ever enjoy spending someone else's money more."

CHAPTER 18

Hayes

STANDING IN OUR HOTEL ROOM, we stare at the single bed in awkward silence. I don't know what's on her mind, but her thoughts might be as dirty as my own, going by the slight blush on her cheeks. All I want to do right now is toss her onto the bed and climb over her, rip her clothes from her body, and savor every morsel of her as I kiss and lick her lips, her neck, her breasts, her pussy —*everything*. My entire body aches thinking of doing just that to her. My cock hardens, my balls throb, and a deep desire washes over me.

After our first night in this competition, I know there's a real chance that we won't survive to the end. And I can't imagine dying without having Lilith one more time.

"You can shower and sleep first; I'll stand watch."

Her eyes cut to me. "And when will you sleep?"

"After you are well rested. We have nothing to do for the next two days but take turns sleeping and looking out for whoever finds us."

She nods and heads into the fancy bathroom. I hear the water run, and all my male instincts want me to open the door and join her. Instead, I distract myself by trying to tap into the hotel security system.

I've just succeeded in pulling up the hotel cameras when the bathroom door opens, and Lilith stands in the doorway, wrapped in nothing but a towel. Her hair is dripping wet, and her lips are parted as steam leaves the bathroom in a haze around her glowing skin. She's so fucking beautiful but so fucking forbidden.

I freeze seeing so much of her naked body, and yet not enough. I want more. And I think there's a tiny part of her that might want more, too.

But she's married.

And she hates me.

And she just lost her sisters and friend.

Sex is the last thing on her mind.

Still, my gaze follows her as she moves from the bathroom to the bed. She climbs into the bed and pulls the covers up before removing the towel and tossing it onto the floor.

I'm rock hard at her nakedness under the covers.

Jesus, what does this woman do to me? Why am I so attracted to her? Is it just because she's now forbidden? Do I enjoy the thrill of the chase that much?

"Everything okay?" she asks, staring at me with a dark intensity I can't quite read.

"Yes, everything is quiet." I hold up my phone so she can see the security cameras I tapped into.

She nods and rolls onto her side, tucking the covers tightly around her.

"You should sleep. I'll wake you if anything happens," I say.

She yawns, and then her eyes flutter shut.

I turn off the lamp, the only light on in the room. And

then I do everything I can to focus on my phone instead of her chest rising and falling under the covers.

She's not mine. She's not mine. She's not mine.

She belongs to Titus. She chose him, not me.

Those words play in my head over and over, but it does nothing to change how badly I need to wrap my body around her naked one.

She rolls one way and then the other, and I realize she's not asleep. She's struggling to fall asleep despite how tired we both are.

"Are you thinking about them?" I say quietly, referring to her sisters and friend.

She pauses her rolling, not answering right away.

"Yes," she breathes in barely whisper. It's an honest word, a tiny piece of her heart exposed to me.

She tucks the covers tighter around her body as if she needs a hug. I wish I could hug her. I wish I could take her pain away. I wish more than anything in the world I could bring them all back for her.

The next words that leave her mouth surprise me. Her voice is still extremely soft and quiet, so much so that I think I might've imagined her speaking to me at all.

"Are you always thinking about her? The woman you all lost?"

I don't know how she knows about Iris or even what she knows exactly. But it doesn't really matter—my answer is the same as hers. "Yes, I'm always thinking about her. I don't think you ever stop thinking about the ones you lose."

She looks at me with heavy eyes full of tears she refuses to release. "No, you don't. You don't ever get over that."

Her words are a stab to my heart. She's talking about me killing her father, and she'll never forgive me for it.

"Do you love him?" I ask, wondering if, in the shadow

of the darkness and with our lives on the line, she'll answer any of my questions honestly.

"Yes," she says immediately. It's not a lie. I can feel the truth in that one word. It's why we're here, in this competition. She loves him and is willing to do anything for him.

Her eyes find me in the darkness and hold my gaze, not yielding.

"Why?" I ask again.

"Because it's the only way..." she trails off. She's so close to answering me, and yet so far still.

"Do you still hate me? Will you always hate me?"

"Yes." And then she turns over, no longer looking at me. For some reason, that single word feels a lot more like a lie than a truth. It seems I softened her a little bit to me when I rescued her. Being here with her has made her like me a little more and hate me a little less.

But it's probably just me reading into it. She hates me. She'll always hate me. I have to accept that, but it doesn't mean I have to hate her too.

I take turns watching the camera and her. My eyes are drawn to her more than the cameras as she finally drifts off to sleep.

I let her sleep all night and into the morning, not caring that my own eyes are starting to grow heavy and my body spasms with the need to sleep. She matters more.

Then I see them—two men so completely out of place in the lobby of the hotel.

"Lilith, wake up!" I shout at her as I grab my weapons and make my way towards the door.

She sits up instantly as if she hadn't been sound asleep seconds ago.

"What is it?" she asks.

"Two men, maybe more. I'm going to deal with them

before they get anywhere near this room. Get dressed and get ready to run."

"Hayes, no—"

But I'm already out the door. I'm not gonna let any of them anywhere near her, not again. I'm not going to let her get kidnapped or play damsel in distress again.

"Don't move," a deep voice says the second I step out of the hotel room. I feel the barrel of a gun pressed against the back of my head. Two other men walk down the hallway toward me.

Fuck.

But I know what I have to do. "I hid the jewel, and only I know where it is. Leave my wife alone, and I'll show you where it is. If you enter that room, if you so much as touch her, I'll never tell you where it is."

"You'll tell us where it is, or we'll blow your brains out."

I shake my head slowly. "I don't care if I die. I only care that she lives."

"Grab the girl. That way, Mr. Lovesick here will do whatever we say."

"If you enter that room, Lilith will press a trigger, and the jewel will be blown to pieces."

"You're lying."

"Try me," I say with a vicious smile.

"If you blow up the jewel, then you are as much a dead man as we are."

"I'll take my chances on finding another jewel before the time is up. All I care about is that she lives."

My heart pounds as one of the men hesitates at the door, not sure whether he should enter or heed my warning.

"If you're lying to us, we'll hunt down your pretty little wife. We'll tie you up and force you to watch while we all have a turn with her. And then we'll make you watch as we blow her brains out. Do you understand?"

I nod. It's all a bluff. Lilith has the jewel, but this way, she'll have a chance at living, at winning the game.

"Tie his arms up," the man in charge says.

His goons tie my arms behind my back before starting to drag me down the hallway. I stare longingly at the door I know Lilith is behind and listening to every word. I hope she runs as far away from here as possible. I hope she wins the game and wins Titus's heart. I hope she avenges her sister and friend's death.

Before tonight is over, these men are going to get revenge for me killing her father.

CHAPTER 19

Lilith

A WILDFIRE of anger rages through my veins as I listen to Hayes on the other side of the door. We knew someone would come for us, but I thought we were in this together. Instead, Hayes decided to go play the hero.

I hear their footsteps retreat down the hall as I palm a knife in my hand. It takes everything in me not to immediately throw open the door and start throwing daggers into their backs, Hayes included.

I compress my fury into a low growl and replay the conversation in my head, looking for any clue as to where Hayes might be leading them.

Mr. Lovesick, they called him. He's not Mr. Lovesick; he's Mr. Dumb-as-Shit for thinking this plan is at all a good idea. His arms are tied behind his back. He doesn't have the jewel. *What crazy fucking plan is this?* He can't survive unless I or someone else comes to his rescue.

I don't care if I die; I care that she lives. That's what the man with the hero complex said. I should let him die just to prove a point.

But then what? Does Hayes really think I can continue this competition without him? We've barely made it a day and a half together. I'd die immediately in the second round without him.

He's a fool—a fucking fool—if he thinks this plan of his is somehow going to save me. It might have saved me today, but it ensured my death tomorrow.

I shouldn't save him. I should leave him to figure out how to get out of this mess on his own. It's clearly what he wants.

I stare down at the black dress I hastily put on after Hayes told me someone was coming. I wish I had real clothes. Any other clothes would be easier to move in instead of this.

With my knife, I slice the bottom of my dress off until it stops mid-thigh, giving me more freedom of movement. I roll my shoulders back and take a deep breath.

Step one—arm myself. I gather every weapon I can find in the hotel room, attaching knives to my body and putting a gun into my purse. I stare at my high heels and decide barefoot is my better bet.

Then I look at the jewel. My dress doesn't have pockets, and I refuse to put it anywhere but on me after everything we've gone through to get it. So I place it in the inside lining of my bra. I can feel the sharp jaggedness of the jewel and will know immediately if it slips out.

My plan cemented in my mind, I pick up my phone and dial the number.

"Hello?" Gage answers with confusion in his voice. I'm sure I'm one of the last people he expected a phone call from.

"Where's Hayes?"

"What do you mean? He's with you, right? That's what Titus said, anyway. You need some private time to mourn the loss of your sisters and friend, and Hayes is your bodyguard."

"You know that isn't true, so stop with the bullshit."

Gage pauses. "Yes, I know you are in a competition to find out who The Abyss is."

"Good, so I don't have to catch you up on much. Tell me where Hayes is."

"Why? What happened?"

I run my hand through my hair in frustration. "Hayes decided to play the goddamn hero instead of working together as a team. He's currently leading his captors astray and away from me, trying to protect me. If I don't find him, they'll kill him."

Silence.

"Gage?"

Another long pause. "Hayes can take care of himself. He doesn't need you saving him."

I growl. "Like hell, he can! They took his weapons. He's tied up, largely outnumbered, and he lied to them. He doesn't have the jewel they're searching for. He's a dead man. I know he's talented. That he can make any woman fall in love with him and spill their secrets immediately, but these are burly criminals we are talking about. He can't flirt or joke his way out of this."

Silence greets me once again, and I almost think Gage hung up on me. "It looks like Hayes is leading them toward an empty warehouse on the west side of town. I'll text you the exact address."

"Thank you," I exhale.

"I was wrong," Gage says suddenly.

"What do you mean? Is Hayes not headed toward the warehouse?" My heart stops.

"No, he is. I just meant he might need your help after all."

"No shit he does."

Gage chuckles. "Good luck." And then he hangs up the phone.

I'm already running out of the hotel room to the elevators while I call a car service to pick me up, no longer caring that others could track me easily if I use my own credit cards.

The drive is long, almost forty-five minutes. Hayes is clearly leading them as far away from me as he possibly can.

I shake my head as my rage simmers through me. I'm going to ring his neck for this, for risking everything because he thinks he knows better.

"Are you sure this is your stop?" The driver asks, eyeing the run-down building.

I stare out the window. There is no obvious sign of Hayes, but I feel it deep in my bones that this is where Hayes would lead them. Somewhere abandoned. Somewhere where innocents won't get killed.

"Yes, this is my stop." I get out of the car, trying to reconcile the man I know with a man who would kill my father. My father was innocent. There had to be a reason Hayes killed him. He doesn't kill anyone who doesn't deserve it.

A chill races through me at that thought. *Who was the guilty party? Hayes or my father?*

I shake off those questions. I have to save Hayes first, then get him to tell me the truth.

The car speeds off the second I step out, as if he knows a fight is about to break out here.

I pull a blade and my gun out as I creep toward the building. Walking along the side of the building, I look for any way in that would go undetected. I find broken windows on the east side when I hear the voices.

I freeze, afraid if I breathe too loudly, they'll hear me.

"Where is it? We're growing tired of your games, boy."

Hayes chuckles. "You can grow tired all you want. But patience is a virtue."

"Your wife is dead if you don't show us the jewel in the next three minutes. We've had someone on her this entire time, waiting in the shadows. If you don't give us the jewel, he'll blow her brains out."

Hayes laughs. "No, you don't. You're a terrible liar."

The man hisses at Hayes. "Try me, you hopeless romantic fool. Try me and see what happens to your girl."

"My girl is perfectly safe. Because I, unlike you, do have eyes on her."

I frown. *That has to be a bluff, right?* They are both liars. No one has eyes on me because I'm right here, listening to this stupid conversation.

I stare into the broken glass and can make out Hayes's face. He looks calm and relaxed, completely in control. Or he's accepted that he's about to die and is okay with it. But he doesn't look hurt. His hands are still tied behind his back, and several guns are pointed at his head.

Fuck, how do I rescue him without one of them pulling a trigger? And how do I ensure I kill every single one so no one knows my talents after this?

Hayes's eyes meet mine in the reflection of the broken glass. His jaw clenches, and he frowns at me.

I glare back at him.

He shakes his head subtly, urging me to leave.

I silently snarl back. *You don't get to tell me what to do. I'm the boss. You answer to me.*

He huffs and turns his attention away from me so he doesn't draw the attention of the others to my position. But I can see the vein popping out on the side of his neck. His body tenses, and he grinds his teeth together.

Hayes is angry with me, but he doesn't get to be angry with me. I get to be angry with him.

After assessing the situation, I decide my best bet is to attack from the rafters. That way, they won't know how many or who is attacking them. And I'll have the advantage of being able to see them all.

I find a fire escape and begin climbing, listening carefully for the sound of bullets firing or a fight breaking out, anything that tells me my time has run out.

Near the top of the building, I climb in through a small open window and find a beam to pull myself up on if I can reach it. I test how far away it is, but I'm going to have to jump to reach it. And then rely entirely on my arm strength to pull myself up.

It's a gamble. I could make it or just as easily fall to my death.

I stare down and see Hayes being shoved forward as one of the men yells in his face. He's going to die if I don't do something soon.

Without putting any more thought into it, I fling myself for the beam. My fingers barely catch as my body swings back and forth. Burning fills my biceps as I use all of my strength to hold on.

"You're a dead man!" The man in charge pulls out his gun and aims it at Hayes's head.

Fuck.

I swing my legs as hard as I can and pull with all of my might until I get a leg over the beam. I pull my gun out of my pocket and aim it at the man in charge, firing at the back of his head before he can pull the trigger first.

After my gunshot ceases, no one speaks, shocked at what just happened. The man drops to his knees and falls face-first to the floor—dead.

The men start shouting at each other, waving their guns around. Some race toward the doors and windows, but others aim up, looking for me. I ignore all but the two that still have their guns locked on Hayes.

I fire two shots in quick succession. One hits my target between the eyes, and he falls, but the other only hits his shoulder. He raises his gun again, and I know he's going to fire at Hayes.

I grab a dagger, knowing my aim is better with daggers than a gun, and fling it at his wrist. It drives into his skin at the intersection of his wrist and thumb, forcing him to drop the gun. It gives me time to send another dagger into his heart.

Hayes spots me, his gaze unnerving as he watches me with stoic awe on his face.

You're mine, I mouth to him.

He nods once. Then he charges toward a man who has spotted me and aimed a gun in my direction. A bullet flies at me, and I duck just in the nick of time as Hayes drives his shoulder into the stomach of the man, tackling him to the ground.

I shoot back quickly, hitting the man in the head before he pulls a weapon on Hayes. With Hayes safe, I turn my attention to the other men in the room.

Fire, fire, fire...I shoot, hitting each target in the chest. I don't trust my aim enough to aim for their heads, even if I get lucky once in a while.

I duck another barrage of bullets invading the rafters where I crouch. I grip my gun, knowing I have limited bullets left. My daggers are in even lower supply.

The second there is a pause in the firing, I lift my head enough to aim for where most of the bullets were coming from and fire off two shots.

"Drop your weapons and come down now, or your hubby is a dead man," a deep, growly voice shouts from below.

Lying flat on the beam, I peer down to see the truth of his words. Hayes has five men surrounding him, and all of them have their guns aimed at him. I can't possibly take them all out before one of them gets a bullet off.

"Come down, princess, without your weapons."

"Don't," Hayes says—a single word.

Don't listen to him. Don't save me. I'm going to die anyway. I was always going to die at the end of this. Save yourself.

Don't.

I never listened to words like don't. I've always risen to a challenge.

You're mine, Hayes. Mine to do what I want with. Mine to decide your fate, not them. You don't get to die tonight. You don't get to die without giving me answers. You don't get to die unless I say so.

I empty my gun of the bullets, dropping them one by one to the ground. Then I release the gun; it hits the floor with a heavy thud.

"Good girl. Now climb down," the voice says.

I climb back out through the window and slide down the fire escape. With my hands up, I enter the warehouse.

"Now, tell your accomplices to come down," the man with a scruffy dark beard and a large frame says.

"Accomplices?" I cock my head to the side. My gaze flicks to Hayes, who is shaking his head at me with a smirk on his face.

"You think she has accomplices? Are you insane or just a fool?" Hayes says.

"You're the only fool here, and you're about to be dead. So I'd shut my mouth if I were you," the bearded man says.

Hayes raises his eyebrow at me as if to say he's going to enjoy watching me kill them.

I smirk and acknowledge the metal touch against my

skin—the daggers I stuck in the back of my dress. I assess the scene with as much confidence as I can muster. I know I can do this, but Hayes better be smart enough to get out of the way of any bullets coming his way.

With the way Hayes's eyes are glowing, he's ready for me to make my move and show these assholes who I am and what I'm capable of. I don't need any accomplices. Their friends were all killed by one woman, a woman they vastly underestimated. It will be the last thing they learn before they die.

CHAPTER 20

Hayes

THEY'RE fools for not realizing what Lilith is capable of. For not realizing that all the bullets were coming from a single spot. That she acted alone. And they are going to pay the ultimate price for it.

Even I underestimated her. She's improved her skills. Her shots are more accurate than ever before. Her strength and bravery surprised me, even though it shouldn't have. I don't know how I didn't realize how fierce she is the second I met her. She's not in need of saving. She's in need of a partner—her equal. One who is as strong as her.

Titus—he's her partner, her equal. It's no surprise she fell for him, and he for her.

And it's why I will always yearn for her and follow her around with puppy dog eyes until she finally decides to put me out of my misery.

But it doesn't stop me from being pissed at her. She should have let me deal with this, even if it meant my own death. She should have let me go.

Lilith's eyes glow with a rage I've never seen before. And she's been angry enough times for me to know that what she looks like when she's pissed. This is different. She's let herself feel all of her anger, harnessing it into the fight ahead.

Her eyes cut to me, a signal to move now.

I duck at the same time she throws three daggers in rapid succession. With my arms tied behind my back, I'm not as agile as I'd like to be. And I can't do much to fight against the others, but I charge toward the man nearest to Lilith, distracting him as a dagger slices into his chest.

It was a mistake. The guy to my right and furthest from Lilith comes running at me. He has two knives in his hands instead of a gun. Lilith can't do anything to kill him as my body is blocking her view.

I square off toward him, driving my feet into the ground. Waiting, waiting...and then a slice of pain comes, and I spin us until his back is facing Lilith.

His blue eyes bulge as a dagger hits him in the back, he gulps for air, and then he slides down to the floor.

I breathe heavily as I stare at Lilith standing casually in front of me, like she's barely broken a sweat.

When she meets my eyes, her jaw clenches, her brows furrow, and her nostrils flare. She grips one remaining dagger, and for a moment, I think she's going to fling the dagger into my own chest.

"I'm in charge, not you," she says.

"I'm in charge of keeping you safe. And sometimes that means not getting your permission first when your life is on the line."

"I was never in danger."

"You were."

She growls. "That's not your decision to make."

"I wasn't in any real danger either. That wasn't your decision to make to come rescue me."

"You weren't in any real danger? Really? You had a dozen men with guns dragging you around with your arms tied behind your back. You were completely defenseless," she yells at me.

"That doesn't mean I was in danger. Just because I couldn't rescue myself doesn't mean I was in danger. Danger means fear. It means I'm afraid to be injured or die. I'm afraid of neither."

"You're a fool."

I nod. *I am a fool—a fool who fell in love with the wrong girl. A girl who would never, ever be mine. A woman worth so much more than I could ever deserve.*

She walks toward me, eyeing the blood on my neck.

"How bad?" she asks.

"It's not going to kill me."

She gives me a look meant to kill me.

I laugh, which earns me another look.

She grabs my neck, and my body screams in pain. I grind my teeth together to keep from yelling out. There is no way I'm going to tell her to stop touching me.

She inspects my wound. Deciding it's not fatal, she scans the rest of my body. Her hands run over my shoulders, chest, and waist. When she goes lower, I raise my eyebrow at her and smirk.

"You should definitely check in my pants. I'm pretty sure I was stabbed in the groin. Check for bleeding. You might need to suck the blood off."

She rolls her eyes at me, but I swear she huffs out a painful breath of relief. Maybe she actually cares if I live or die.

"Hey," I say, and her eyes cut up to me. "I'm fine. Really. And if I wasn't, it would be my fault, not yours."

"As if I care."

My lips curl because I know she cares. Her feelings toward me and her need for answers are the only things keeping me alive.

"Care to untie me?" I nod toward where my hands are still tied behind my back.

She stares at me, a thought clearly creeping through her head. "No, not until you've been thoroughly punished for disobeying first."

I raise my brows. "While I'm all for you punishing me however you see fit, don't you think you should untie me so we can get somewhere safe first? By my count, we have a little less than twenty-four hours to keep the jewel and stay alive."

"We do need to get somewhere safe, but I need to make sure you don't do anything foolish like this ever again." Her voice is a sultry tease, and it sends delightful chills through my body.

"I'm yours, Lily. Yours to punish, to do with as you please."

She grins wickedly. "Good. Let's find a place with a little less blood before I spill yours."

CHAPTER 21

Hayes

WE STEP into the cheap motel room, having scrounged enough cash from the dead men's wallets to pay for a single night. That's all we have left to survive the first round: one night and day in this room.

Looking around, this room is far worse than the other one we stayed in, where all of our stuff still sits untouched. I know Lilith is dying to get out of her dress, and what's left of my suit is ripped and covered in blood. But there is no getting out of the suit, not without Lilith's permission.

My arms are still tied behind my back with a zip tie. While I could try to get out of it, it would hurt like hell, and Lilith would kick my ass for not following her orders. So, the zip tie stays until Lilith removes it.

Lilith piles the weapons she gathered onto a small desk. Based on the number of weapons, she could defend us for days.

"Where do you want me, boss?" I ask.

Her lips curl slightly as I say the word 'boss,' and I know I've worked a little of my charm on her. She takes a deep breath and collapses onto the couch, causing it to creak and pop.

She's exhausted, and I'm equally as tired. The adrenaline that was coursing through her veins earlier is long gone. All that's left in her is cortisol and fatigue.

For a second, I think she's going to fall asleep when she closes her eyes. Maybe she's forgotten all about me, but then she stands suddenly.

"Unzip me," she says.

I raise an eyebrow. "Kind of hard to do with the...you know."

"You could unzip a woman's dress blind with your arms cut off and nothing but your teeth to undo the zipper and bra with. So don't try to get out of the zip ties. It won't work."

I huff. "Come here, then."

She walks to me and positions her back to mine. My hands nestle up against her ass, and I squeeze my eyes shut at the feel of her warm body in my hands.

"Stop it and focus. Zipper," she snaps.

I grin and only half obey her orders. Bending over, my fingers dance up her spine as I find the zipper. Then I let my hands skim her bare skin as I slowly lower the zipper. Soon I feel the upper curve of her ass again.

"Thank you," she breathes, seemingly lost in my touch. She takes a step away from me, and my hands feel empty once again.

I take a deep breath, completely clueless as to what to do with her. I told her I'd make her fall in love with me and that I want to fuck with her, but I don't think she'll ever fall for me ever again. She loves Titus. I'm just her plaything, so I won't feel guilty for playing in return.

When I open my eyes, Lilith is sitting naked on the couch.

My eyes bulge. "What are you doing?"

"Getting comfortable. That dress is scratchy and makes it hard for me to breathe."

"You being naked makes it hard for me to breathe."

She laughs manically, like it was her intention to see me in pain.

"You could put a towel on or get into bed and sleep."

"Hmm, I could. But that would make it hard for me to punish you."

Jesus fucking Christ. She's going to punish me naked. She really does know my weak spots.

I take a deep breath and look her in the eyes, ignoring how her loose red curls spill over the top of her breasts. I ignore her hardened nipples, straining in my direction. I ignore her spread legs, giving me a clear view of her pink pussy lips. Yes, I definitely keep my focus on her eyes and not her luscious, delicious body.

Her lips are pursed, and her eyes intense as she watches me.

"Kneel," she says.

I gulp. *I'm going to die. Whatever she has planned, this is how I die: kneeling in front of the most beautiful, badass woman I've ever met, naked before me, but not mine to touch. It is the perfect way to die, I guess.*

I kneel before her, and her legs spread wider. This time, I don't try to tear my gaze away from her nakedness—it's hopeless. I stare right between her legs, licking my lips like she's about to be my dessert.

Lilith waits, not giving me another instruction. As soon as my mouth starts to salivate, I realize exactly what my punishment is. I can look but not touch. She's going to dangle everything I want in front of me and deny me. And I might deserve it, but it's going to be the worst kind of torture.

"Kiss me, here," she says, pointing to a spot on her inner thigh, just past her knee.

I swallow hard, the anticipation killing me as I realize she is going to let me taste her. *Thank fucking god, I would die without at least tasting her skin again.*

I lean forward, my lips puckering as I lean down between her thin, muscular thighs and kiss the scrumptious spot next to her finger.

Fuck me. I make the mistake of taking a deep breath as my lips brush against her soft, warm skin. She smells like honeysuckle and lavender—sweet and intoxicating. She smells like *mine.*

I squeeze my eyes shut, like that is somehow going to stop her scent from entering my nostrils. But turning off my vision only makes my sense of smell stronger.

I drag my face away, my lips brushing more of her leg before I finally pull away. When I do, I open my eyes and find a devilish smirk on her face. She knows she has me. She knows what her body does to me. She knows she's my weakness. Despite everything, her body is like a drug to me. It makes me a slave to my feelings toward her. There is no hiding how I feel, not in this moment. I might as well be naked, too.

"And here," she says, pointing to the same spot on her other thigh.

I take a deep breath and then kiss her in that spot. This time, her overwhelming scent doesn't draw me in, but the warmth and softness of her perfectly muscled skin sends heat flooding into my body.

I lean back on my heels, torn between getting as far away from her as possible and just leaning into this and taking whatever scraps she'll allow me to have.

She touches a spot on her stomach. "Here."

I bite my lip, knowing how much this is going to hurt,

when she tells me to stop. Ultimately, I decide it's best to lean into this and enjoy every second until that pain comes.

I inch forward on my knees between her spread legs, until I can reach the spot on her taunt stomach. When my lips land on her skin, I feel her pulse. It's rapid and pulling the heat off her body south.

I grin at her, knowing her secret as much as she knows mine. She chose Titus and wants a lifetime with him. She may even be in love with Titus, but he isn't here. And she has needs, and we have history.

I'm sure Titus is more than adept in the bedroom, but I know what we were like together. I know how explosive, how fucking hot we were. And right now, she burns as badly as I do to have that feeling again. Oh, she'll deny herself. She has too much integrity, and she wants to punish me too badly, but she wants me—desperately.

She grins right back. Our lust has become a weapon we each wield at the other.

"Here." She touches the curve of her breast.

I lick my lips, dying to taste her. I move closer between her spread legs and dip down, sweeping my tongue across the sensitive flesh just an inch away from her puckered nipple.

She arches her back slightly, moving her body closer to mine and spreading her legs wider.

"Here." She points to the same spot on her other breast.

With my darkened eyes hooded in her direction, I run my tongue over the spot she indicated and let it slip further south, to her hardened nipple. I suck furiously and lap over the sensitive flesh.

For one second, her hands dig into my hair, holding me to that spot and relishing in the desire flooding our bodies. Then, in the next second, she's yanking me away and slapping me hard across my face.

"Disobey again, and I'll mark the other side of your pretty face, sunshine."

"Mmm, I think I'd enjoy that."

She tugs on my hair roughly. "I think you would."

"Do your worst, vicious one."

She shakes her head at me in apparent disbelief. *How did she fall in love with me?*

"Here." She touches a sensitive spot on her neck, one I know will send chills and shockwaves through her body.

I rake my teeth over my bottom lip in heavy anticipation. I climb up her body as best as I can with my arms still tied behind my back. It's pure torture, since I want to grab onto her body and feel her warm flesh in my hands. She yanks up on my hair, pulling me to exactly the spot she wants me to kiss.

Kneeling has become a drape of my hardened body against hers as I reach the spot on her neck with my lips.

"I want you," I whisper as I kiss the spot on her neck.

Before she asks, I kiss the same spot on the other side. "And I know you want me too."

A soft moan escapes her lips, and her dazed eyes meet mine.

Say yes, say you want me. Put an end to this suffering, and just let me fuck you. Let me pleasure you, vicious one.

But Lilith is stronger than I am. She's so fucking strong.

Before I realize what she's reaching for, I feel a sharp, coldness of a metal blade against my throat.

"You're a fool if you think I'll fall for your antics ever again."

I grin, cocking my head and letting my skin brush against the blade until I feel a trickle of blood oozing out.

"Yes, I'm a fool. But that doesn't mean I don't know exactly what you want. It doesn't mean I don't know every inch of your body. I know how to make you feel good. I know how to make you feel alive. I know how to push out those dark shadows under your eyes from everything you've been through lately. Let me help you, not because I need you, but because you deserve a release."

Shaking her head, she slices the knife across my neck in a shallow cut.

My flesh stings from the flesh wound. But it's not until she lowers her lips to my skin that I feel real pain.

She kisses my skin harshly, not caring that my blood is smearing over her lips. Then she yanks me harshly away from her by my hair.

"You belong to me, Hayes Rollins. From right now until your dying breath, you are mine. You are to follow my orders without arguing. You are to do exactly what I say when I say it. You will not go rogue ever again. You will be my obedient servant. And when this game is over, you will answer every question I have truthfully because you belong to me. Do I make myself clear?"

"Yes, boss."

Her eyes narrow at me, but all I can see is my blood on her lips. My eyes trail over her body, unabashedly clear of how attractive I find her. They linger over every curve of her body until I spot between her legs again that are spread so fucking wide for me. I see her arousal; how fucking wet she is for me. It's spilling out of her.

I groan, knowing she's not going to let me have her. Lingering tastes are all I'm ever going to get. This moment may be the last time I ever get her like this at all. It may be the last time I ever get to see how badly she wants me and yet denies both of us what we want.

"Here," she says.

I drag my eyes up, unsure of where she's going to let me kiss her. Shock hits me as I see where she's pointing: those red lips, marked with my blood.

I won't survive this. The pain of really tasting her and not having her is going to cause me to have a heart attack right here. At least I'll die getting to kiss her one last time.

The room stills as I rise on my heels to reach her lips. My body brushes against hers in every way. I've never wished I was naked more than I do right now.

Even though I can feel her warm, welcoming body against me, it's not enough—not nearly enough. I want to feel her skin against skin. I want my cock nestled between her legs until I can feel her wetness spill over me. I want to feel her pebbled nipples against my chest and her sharp nails digging into my back.

My lips hover over hers, knowing this is a turning point in her twisted game. I don't know what she has planned next, but I know it will cost me a body part or two, including my heart.

She raises her eyebrows, questioning my hesitation. No way in hell am I refusing to kiss her, just savoring this blissful moment. Bliss turns to hell when my lips brush against hers, though. I must have died and gone to hell because she tastes like hot flames against my tongue. She alone has the power in those flames to destroy me.

CHAPTER 22

Lilith

THE SECOND HAYES'S lips touch mine I know deep in my soul that I've made a huge error. I thought I was strong enough to deny myself him in order to punish him. This is as much about proving to both of us that he has no power over me anymore as it is about punishing him. But I was wrong—I'm not strong enough.

I'm not strong enough.

I'm not strong enough.

I'm not strong enough...

I grab his neck, pulling him hard against me as our lips smash together, and our tongues tangle. Blood smears against my hands from his wounds. I close my eyes as the world becomes fuzzy around the edges, and the charge in my body intensifies.

Fuck, I need this. Fuck everything else. I need him—now.

My legs wrap around his waist, holding him in place as my hands grip his neck tighter. A moan rips through my body. Then Hayes fully attacks me with his lips and rocks his hips into me as my body tightens around him.

Rage twists into desire as I try to pull him closer and

closer to me. *Damn him and his clothes. Or was it my choice to keep his clothes on? Why didn't I tell him to remove his clothes?*

I start tugging at his shirt, and he chuckles against my lips, the scruff on his sharp jawline rubbing against my cheek. Chills race through my body like a wildfire as I rip the buttons off his shirt. I don't care if it's the only clothes he has to wear right now. *None of this is smart,* something says deep in my brain, but I ignore that voice and listen to the stronger voice telling me to fuck him. *Fuck him over and over and over and never let him go. He's yours. Hayes is yours. Yours to do as you please with. To fuck, to boss around, to want, to love, to kill—an endless amount of possibilities for this man.*

I start to yank his shirt off his shoulders before I remember his arms are tied behind his back.

"Are you going to untie me now? I know you can't wait to feel my hands on your body again, Lily."

I growl, my body shivering at his name for me. But there is no way I'm going to untie him. That would mean I caved and that this isn't actually punishment for him. He would have some control back, and I'll never give him control over me again—not my body and definitely not my heart.

He sighs. "I'll only touch you when you say, I promise."

I shake my head. "No."

Then I drop from him and shove his chest back.

He misunderstands my action and begins to stumble back away from me, thinking I'm telling him that I'm not going to let us act on this uncontrollable desire between us.

"Where are you going?" I snap at him in a heady voice.

He swallows hard. "Uh...I'm..."

I smirk, grabbing onto the waistband of his pants and yanking him to me. "I love it when I make you speechless."

A deep chuckle is his response.

I undo the button and zipper of his pants, his hooded

eyes locked on my hands as they work. Neither of us breathes as I finally get his pants open and begin sliding them down his thighs.

I suck in a shallow breath when his glorious cock springs free, and his piercing catches my attention. Taking in how long and hard he is, I rethink my goals.

My intention was to make him suffer. To make him want me and then deny him. To make him so painfully hard and not give him the use of his hands to do anything about it. To make him sleep with a hard erection that he couldn't relieve.

He steps out of the pants, watching me watch him.

I rake my teeth over my bottom lip, trying to decide if I want to bite him, suck him, or just climb on top of him. My eyes slowly rake up his body until our eyes meet. There's a glow in his eyes that tells me he can read my mind.

"On your knees," I say after sitting on the couch in front of him.

"With pleasure," he grins as he kneels before me, this time both of us naked. His shoulders roll back as his arms are still tied behind his back. His hair falls loosely out of his bun, hanging down onto his shoulders and covering the wounds on his neck.

My breath catches in my throat as I look at him, so eager to please between my legs. He's everything I ever wanted and everything capable of destroying me. I fear him more than the men hunting us for the jewel.

I take a deep, shuttering breath as he watches me, waiting for me to give him another command like the good little pet he is.

My eyes skim over the tattoos, the muscles, the hardness of his body. I want every inch of him.

"Any day now, boss," he says with a smirk.

I narrow my eyes and grind my teeth together. "Here." I

point to the sensitive spot between my legs. "Lick me here, pet."

He laughs at my new nickname for him.

"Gladly," he says as his eyes darken with lust.

He wastes no time, lowering his head to between my thighs. He shoves my thighs apart with the sides of his face as his tongue sweeps up my slit.

Holy fucking god!

I almost came from the single lick of his tongue. He's too much, too fucking much, and not enough at the same time.

My body arches, and a sharp gasp of air spills from my lips. The damn bastard grins wider than I've seen him grin in a long time at the reaction he stoked in me.

"Bastard," I curse.

"Your fucking bastard."

His words almost have me undone—*yours*.

I shiver.

"Did I tell you to stop?" I bark.

He chuckles and sweeps his tongue over my slit again and again. I grip the couch cushions I'm sitting on, trying to distance myself from this man and the pleasure he's bringing me. He's just doing it because I told him to, and I only did that because he's damn good in bed. Sex is how he manipulates women—how he gets what he wants. This is all an act. He's playing me, I remind myself. I have to play him right back.

"More," I say, remembering my role. I can still do what I planned to do. I can get him to fuck me with his tongue and bring me pleasure—then deny him. Yes, that's what I'll do.

His tongue stops on my clit, circling so fucking slowly.

"Faster," I huff.

He moves his tongue faster, and I swallow down the intensity of it as it floods my body. *How is he so good at this?*

And then I remember again—he's the Retribution Kings's whore. This is his job to be good at it.

I push those thoughts out of my head. *He's not their anything; he's mine.*

I mumble something, but I'm not sure it's a coherent order.

I feel that damn grin of his against my sensitive flesh, and then he bites down on my clit before sending his tongue deep between the wetness of my folds and inside me.

I bite my lip to keep from screaming and continue to grip the cushions like my life depends on it.

And then he stops. I know exactly what he's doing. He's doling out his own punishment under the guise of just following my orders.

My dark eyes meet his. He raises an eyebrow in a question. *What do you want from me? Tell me that you want me. Tell me that you're mine as mine as I'm yours. Tell me that you still want me despite everything I've done to you.*

I cool my features and say, "Don't stop until you've made me come. Twice."

He licks his bottom lip, and then without a word, his tongue sweeps over my clit.

I convulse and come.

My body shatters at the single touch of his hot tongue on my body.

I don't know what sounds leave my mouth. I know that I don't scream his name, but whatever I do say is intense all the same.

He slows his movements as my body comes down from its high. My eyes drift shut, and all I want to do is sleep.

"Uh-huh, I have another orgasm to give you. Boss's orders," he grins against me.

I realize my legs have squeezed shut as he kisses and nudges them apart. I'm beginning to regret my order, not sure if I'm ready for another orgasm so soon. But the gleam in his eyes is enough that I don't want to back down. I won't take it back, and he knows it. He knows exactly what he's doing.

Instead of starting slow, he dives right back in between my wet folds. My overly sensitive clit takes the brunt of the intensity as his tongue licks over me again.

And then my hands leave those cushions. I try to remind myself not to, that I'll regret it later, but I can't stop. My hands grip his hair now, holding on for dear life as his tongue swirls, his teeth nip, and his hot breath warms over my body.

Fuck, I'm so totally fucked.

"More, more, more," I purr.

His tongue dips into me, filling me, but it's not what I really want, I realize.

No, after this orgasm, I'll be good. It will be enough. I'll be able to let go.

I hold his head against my body between my legs, as he groans at my sweet taste filling his mouth.

"You taste so damn good," he breathes out between licks.

"Enough talking. I deserve another orgasm."

He chuckles. "You deserve a lot more orgasms. I want to make you come again and again until you're barely cognizant in the morning."

"Hmm, yes."

And then his tongue is like a brand against my clit, and I'm coming once again.

This time when I scream, I scream his fucking name. I scream it like a lover and a curse and an enemy. I scream it like I hate him and want him and love him and want him dead.

When I'm done screaming, when he's drained me of

another orgasm, he stops. His face rests against the sensitive spot between my legs, not moving and waiting for my next command.

I know the mistake I'm about to make, and I don't fucking care.

"On the couch," I say.

He pauses for just a second, like he can't believe my words. And then he's sitting on the couch next to me, his tied arms pulling tightly behind his back as he sits on his hands. It can't be comfortable for him, but he doesn't seem to mind.

Silence stretches between us as we both breathe heavily.

"Don't fucking move. You're mine," I whisper the words.

He stills, frozen as a statue obeying my orders.

Slowly, I stand and face him. My eyes drag down from his eyes to that cock—that cock I've missed so much.

You're going to regret this, I tell myself.

But I climb onto his lap anyway, and I feel him still even more. My hips hover over his lap as my fingers trail up his abs and chest, barely grazing his skin as I do.

What am I doing? The part of my brain that still works shouts at me. But I can barely hear it; it's so faint.

My hips lower onto his lap, and I feel his hard erection slide between my cheeks as I straddle him.

Hayes's hooded eyes watch me, but he doesn't move. His chest doesn't even rise and fall because he's holding his breath. He's as terrified of what I'm about to do next as I am.

We both need this. It's become a need, not a want. This isn't a punishment; it's a need.

I lean down, suspending my lips over his. Our eyes stare into each other, trying to read what the other isn't saying.

I swallow for what feels like the last time, and then I let

my lips fall onto his. We move at the exact same time, kissing each other like it's our only lifeline we have to breathe.

I sweep my tongue into his mouth as his taunts me back. Wetness pours out of me as the kiss intensifies and spills onto his cock, still positioned between my legs.

"Please," he whimpers when I come up for air, my forehead resting on his.

I should deny him, but that would mean denying me. And I won't live without this.

Silently, I give him my answer. I raise my hips just enough for his cock to angle up, and then I slide my body onto his massive hardness.

I wince at the fullness as he begins to enter me, but Hayes peppers kisses along my jawline, and the pain vanishes. Instead, I'm filled with his hot body inside mine and that piercing hitting deep inside my core.

We both groan as I rock up and down on his cock. My hands grip his shoulders as our bodies glide together.

Other than his eyes, Hayes doesn't move, still following the last order I gave him.

Good, this is about what I want, not him. This is about me using him like he's used me.

"Fuck you," I say, riding him.

There's a tiny gleam in his eyes, but he still doesn't say anything or move a muscle.

"Fuck you for treating me like your mission." I ride him harder.

"Fuck you for lying to me." I dig my nails into his shoulders as I rock up and down on his cock.

"Fuck you for killing my father." I grind my teeth together at that, and I swear there's a look of remorse in his eyes, but he still doesn't move or say anything.

"Fuck you for not telling me what happened." The words keep spilling out and out of me. I can't stop them.

Even the groans and whimpers that leave my lips as my orgasm nears don't stop the words. Out and out and out. It's cathartic to get the words out when he's completely obedient to me. He won't defy me; he's mine to use.

And yet, I shouldn't be doing any of it. But I keep going anyway.

"Fuck you for saving me. I would have died. I couldn't escape those men. I had no plan, no means of escape. You should have let me die."

Hayes's eyes widen. He wasn't expecting me to say that, to admit that I'm weak when all I ever do is say I'm strong and don't need him. But I would have died without him. Maybe that would have been easier.

Still, Hayes keeps his mouth shut. He lets me use him. I don't know if I'm angry or relieved that he doesn't fight me. He doesn't tell me I'm wrong, that I would have survived, that I am strong enough.

"Fuck you for protecting me again by going rogue and letting them take you instead of me."

I lean down and suck his bottom lip into my mouth. I bite down hard until I taste the warm, metallic taste of his blood.

Hayes lets me. He takes it. Doesn't so much as flinch at the drop of pain I caused him. Doesn't yield. Doesn't fight. But his cock is still hard inside me. He's still very much alive. Very much with me. Very much wants me.

I pause, needing to catch my breath and needing something that I haven't even admitted to myself. Something more. Something...

Hayes nods, or at least I think he does. It's barely a movement, so subtle that I could have just imagined it.

I stare at him.

He stares at me.

And then I thrust up and down on his cock again,

letting his warm, hard body fill the void inside me. I let all my emotions go, but my desire to orgasm on top of this man. I'm frantic as I fuck him. We move so quickly that we're both panting, both so close to releasing everything pent up inside of us.

"Fuck you for putting yourself in danger," I whisper.

He blinks.

I pause for just a second, needing to get the last words out. They're words I can never take back.

"Fuck you because I wasn't sure if I could save you. And if you died..." I swallow. "If you died, I'd die too."

I resume pounding my body on his, not letting either of us process those words or emotions. It's as close as he's going to get to me laying my heart out on the line again for him anytime soon.

But every word was the truth. The fear I felt when he left. The fear I felt when I saw how many men there were and how close the guns were to his head. The fear when I didn't think I could save him. I need him.

"You're mine," I shout, exploding on his cock as my lips brush over his.

He groans, and I feel his warm cum fill me. "You're mine, too," he whispers.

Or did I imagine his words?

The aftershocks of that orgasm wash through both of us, and we shutter before I gently raise my hips as he slides out of me. Otherwise, I don't move from where I'm straddling him.

I don't shy away from this intimate moment, and neither does Hayes.

For once, we don't need words. We just look at each other, and we know. We know how we feel. It's forbidden for so many reasons; this can't happen. And I'll never forgive him for everything he's done.

And yet, for a second, I think I already did. I believe there is more to his story. More to what happened than I know. More he isn't telling me. More he'll tell me soon enough.

I trust him.

Fuck, I trust him.

I want him.

I love him.

Fuck.

I don't say those words out loud. But I know Hayes feels them as much as I feel the same words from him.

He trusts me.

He wants me.

He loves me.

Fuck.

A wry smile curls up both of our lips, thinking the same thing.

Then my phone buzzes from inside my clutch. We both stare at the bag until I slowly inch off of him, my muscles sore from straddling him for so long.

I'm not sure what I'm expecting to see when I grab my phone—maybe another message from The Abyss. But what I find is a message from Titus asking me how I am, telling me he misses me and that he can't wait to have me back in his arms.

"What is it?" Hayes asks, reading my expression.

"Titus," I say, looking at my phone with guilt marring my face.

Hayes frowns and then stands, looking at the message over my shoulder. Then he says words that strike against my heart.

"It's okay. You can tell Titus what happened. You can tell him it was my fault because it is. Tell him once you're done winning the game with me, you'll kill me."

CHAPTER 23

Hayes

MY WORDS CRUSH HER. Her entire demeanor changes the second I finish speaking. She hates my words, and she hates me.

Good, hate me. It's better than loving me.

I told her I'd make her fall in love with me again. It was a fun game. A distraction really from our true feelings. But now that she's basically admitted her feelings about me, I wish I had never started that game.

Lilith can't love me. I'll destroy her. Loving Titus is the only thing that can protect her. I'm a dead man. If she chooses me, she'll end up dead too. She admitted as much.

She glares at me but doesn't respond to what I said. She just looks at me, as if she's waiting for me to take all my words back and tell her the truth.

But my words were the truth. My words were exactly what I needed to say to her, what we both needed to hear. There is no world where we end up together.

And Titus will find out about what happened here. I don't know how exactly, but he will. I will take all the blame. I'll tell him I forced her. I'll ensure that he kills me for what I did. It's better this way. As much as Lilith says she wants to kill me, she won't. When it comes down to it, she can't, I realize.

She loves me. She can't kill me. But she has to, or Titus has to. That was always my fate. Now that I've pissed off Titus enough, he'll have no problem killing me when the time comes.

I pop the zip tie off my wrists, knowing she'll never release me until I take back my words. I refuse to do that. She had her fun bossing me around, but I'd never forgive myself if an attack happened and I was defenseless like that.

She stares at me, not sure what to do with me. I don't know what to do with her either.

"How many hours left until we need to head back to the restaurant?"

"Six," she answers, all back to business and not like my cum is dripping down her thigh. Not like we didn't just shatter each other's world. Not like she just fucked me like no woman has ever fucked me before. I'm ready to die if I can't have her again, because nothing will ever compare to her. No one will ever love me like she does.

"You can shower first," I say.

She shakes her head. "No."

"You want me to shower first?"

"No, I refuse to leave you alone so you can play hero again if someone attacks us."

I frown. "I won't. I promise."

"I don't believe you."

"So what do you suggest? We never shower or leave each other's side ever again?"

"I suggest we shower together if we want to shower. And yes, you're not leaving my side ever again."

I like the sound of that, but I don't admit that out loud.

"You first," she says, gesturing toward the bathroom at the back of the motel.

I'm grinning like a fool until I stop inside the cramped bathroom in major need of a renovation. Rust, grime, and mold overwhelm my nostrils.

I halt so quickly that Lilith slams into my back.

"Why'd you stop?"

"This is the least sexy bathroom in the history of bathrooms."

She scoffs. "It wouldn't matter if this was the sexiest bathroom in the history of bathrooms. I'm not going to fuck you. I've had my fill."

"Right," I say slowly and sarcastically.

She shoves past me, dipping under my arm. She turns the shower on and finds two towels under the sink that will barely cover a thigh, let alone our entire bodies.

Then, we stand silently in the tiny bathroom as the mold invades our nostrils, and we wait for the water to warm up. After five minutes, it's still cold as ice.

"Well, what's your great plan now, boss?"

Her eyes are sharp as ice when she glares at me. "I'm going to shower and get rid of your stench on me." She steps into the cold shower, not shivering or showing any sign of weakness.

Holy fucking hell, do I want her again. I want her more now that I can touch her. I can run my hands up and down her smooth body.

Without thinking, I jump into the shower behind her, the cold of the water not doing a thing to chill the heat that has crept up my body. We stand face to face as the cool water washes over us both. Our eyes heat, and our breaths become heavy in our chests. Suddenly, neither of us is thinking about what I said or what she said. Neither of us care.

Hesitantly, I reach my hand out to her, cupping her chin

as I stroke her cheek. I get in a defensive stance, assuming she's about to slap me, push me away, or pull out a knife from god knows where.

She doesn't.

I suck in a breath as she touches me in the same way back. It's a gentle caress that has me pining for me even more.

"Wash me," she says. For her sake, as much as mine, her hand falls away.

I reach for the bottle of soap on the shelf behind her. As I do, our bodies brush against each other. My cock begins to harden. Her nipples pebble against my chest.

I blow out a slow breath, trying to keep myself from launching myself at her as I pour some of the liquid soap into my hand. There is no washcloth, nothing to help me wash her except my hand.

She sucks in a breath as my hand takes her hand in mine, and I start massaging the soap up her arm. She doesn't blink as she watches my gaze, trying to read me.

I massage the soap into her shoulder, then across her back to her other shoulder and down that arm. I take my time working every tired muscle. When I've finished her arms and hands, I move my hands to her shoulders and slowly work my way down her front.

She doesn't shy away or tell me to stop as I move my suds-covered hands down to her breasts. I take both of them in my hands and feel the fullness of her breasts. I was dying to palm them earlier as they bounced up and down in front of me while she rode me. They feel as glorious as I thought they would. But the way her eyes gleam through the water when I touch her is what I'm really after.

Fuck me, she's beautiful when she doesn't hold back her emotions.

My hands slide down from her breasts over her ab muscles that contract as she sucks in a breath. When I get to her hips, I kneel in front of her, just like she asked me to before.

She raises an eyebrow at me as if reliving that moment only minutes ago.

I smirk. It was the best moment of my life. This is a close second.

I wash down one thigh, then the other. My eyes are glued to the spot between her legs. I want to taste her again. I want to bend her over and fuck her. I want...

It doesn't matter what I want. That can't happen again. It just can't.

Quickly, I stand back up. "Turn around."

She narrows her eyes as if confused as to why I didn't wash between her legs. *Why do I resist my own urges?*

Beats me, sweetheart. I don't know why I do either. But that tiny voice in my head telling me to put an end to this before I do something foolish is the only thing keeping me from fucking her in this cramped shower.

I grab the shampoo, drizzle some into her hair, and then start massaging the suds into her red hair. It starts off innocent enough. It's just hair. This is the least problematic spot I could wash on her. After this, I'll be done. I'll have successfully washed her.

But then a moan—the softest, gentlest moan echoes through the shower.

I stop, my hands caught in her hair. But my cock springs to life like the moan was its calling sound.

She reaches back and strokes my hip as her ass pushes against my cock.

I groan and wrap my arms around her body instinctively. I know I'm not letting her go. Not until this is all over. Not until I'm dead.

"You're playing a dangerous game," I whisper into her ear.

"I like danger, sunshine," she purrs back.

I thrust between her ass cheeks, my cock sliding between the slickness between her legs but not entering her. I have some self-control left; I can stop myself from fucking her.

But then she's arching her back, and her hand reaches down between her legs, gripping my cock like it's hers to command and guiding it to her entrance.

"Fuck me. You know you want to," she whispers.

Suddenly, all my self-control is gone. With one thrust, I'm inside her, and my hands are on her hips.

She gasps as I fill her, her hands pressing against the wall to keep from falling over. Water pours down over us, still frighteningly cold. But the temperature of the water nor the condition of the bathroom make no difference to us.

I sweep her wet hair to the side so I can kiss her neck as I thrust into her again. She smells like the cheap citrus shampoo and mine, fucking mine.

My hands slide up the curves of her sides from her hips to her breasts, drawing another gasp. I need to feel every inch of her that she denied me before. When I palm her breasts, I have every intention of caressing every part of her skin.

"Yes," she moans as I swirl my thumb over her puckered nipple.

I grin against her neck, loving the sound she's making. I need more.

My other hand slides down the front of her body, the water making her skin slick as I find the apex of her thighs.

She tenses as if she can't handle me touching her there and yet wants me to all the same.

"What sound are you going to make, Lily, when I touch you here? Are you going to whimper, moan, gasp, or scream?"

Her breath catches in her throat, and then she's silent.

My cock hardens more in her body, loving the sweet anticipation. I want to bask in this moment forever. I want to tease her over and over, but every moment we spend in here is another moment our enemies could be coming for us. And while I don't mind dying, Lilith deserves to live.

I slide my fingers through the wetness to her clit, rubbing gently over the sensitive nub while waiting for the sounds I know she'll make. But knowing her, she'll probably swallow down any sounds just to deny me.

I grin at that thought, knowing I'll enjoy doing my best work to pull a sound from her, knowing she's doing everything she possibly can to hold back.

I'm right. She's silent as my fingers find her clit. Silent as I thrust harder inside her, while massaging her clit and nipple with my fingers. Silent as I pinch her nipple and then clit. Silent as I fuck her and can feel her orgasm building as her walls tighten around me.

Silent, so fucking silent.

I, on the other hand, am anything but silent. The sounds leaving me more than make up for her silence.

And then we're both coming. My cum pours inside her as her body pulses around me. Her body convulses as her hands press harder against the walls of the shower.

Finally, a sound leaves her lips. It's a bittersweet sound. A sound I love and hate. A sound that scares me. A sound that makes me think she's not going to do what has to be done in the end.

"Hayes," she pants like I'm the only thing that matters in her world. "Hayes..."

CHAPTER 24

Hayes

WE WALK BACK into the restaurant with a minute to spare. We did it. We have the jewel. We survived and weren't attacked again.

But it's eerily quiet, and there isn't anyone else here. We both reach for our weapons, assuming we have entered some sort of trap.

A moment later, the other competitors slowly enter the restaurant, looking just as weary as we feel. No one showed up earlier than they absolutely had to in case we were ambushed at the last second.

No one speaks as the seconds tick by, all of us collectively holding our breath for the timer to run out. But no one comes to try and battle any of us one last time for a jewel. I count the teams in the room to find it's exactly half the number that started.

Our phones vibrate at the same time with another text message from The Abyss.

You made it to the second round. Enjoy your dinner. If you'd like to resign from the game, simply leave anytime during dinner. If you are still seated during dessert, you will be entered into the second round, where half of you will die. Consider carefully.

Lilith raises an eyebrow at me after we both read the message on her phone. We haven't spoken much to each other since she called out my name during our shower sex session. That's probably for the best. Talking, looking, just being near each other—it all leads us to fucking.

We walk to our seats at the table as the six other teams of two do the same. No one leaves immediately, but that doesn't mean that someone won't withdraw over dinner.

I wonder what the next round is and what has enticed so many to enter the game. I consider chatting up the other competitors to get information out of them, but that will only lead to them questioning us as well.

Quiet chatter starts filling the room as wine is poured and an escargot appetizer is brought out. Neither Lilith nor I touch the wine, but we both devour the escargot and breadstick that comes with it.

Lilith stills when she realizes several of the men are eyeing her every movement. We both bought new clothes an hour before coming here. We're much better prepared for the next round in our form-fitting black pants, black jackets, and athletic shoes. Somehow, the men seem more interested in Lilith now than when she was wearing the fancy dress.

"You stole a jewel from Reginald?" a man with piercing blue eyes says to Lilith.

"That was the challenge. Do you have a problem with that...?"

"Jeffrey, and no, no problem. I'm just curious, very curious, about you, Lilith Adler. I think we all are after hearing what happened with Reginald." Jeffrey lifts his gaze to me. "And even more curious about your wife after we heard of your capture, Titus."

Fuck, they know. They know what Lilith did to rescue

me. They know how skilled she is. Her cover is blown. She won't be able to use that element of surprise.

But I have to at least try to convince them they're wrong. I don't know exactly what they know or don't know. But our only chance at Lilith having any advantage is to convince them they got it wrong.

I throw my arm around the back of Lilith's chair and scoff at the crazy idea.

"Lily here wouldn't hurt a fly. But her love for me is so great that the second I was captured, she somehow found the strength to try to help me. It inspired me to fight my way out, and I fell in love with her even deeper." I pause, leaning down and kissing Lilith in an aggressive, sweeping kiss. It pulls at both of us to rehash old feelings, but hopefully, the kiss convinces these assholes we love each other, and Lilith's skills are minimal at best.

Lilith smiles up sweetly at me like I'm her hero, like she's some damsel in distress. Her look is the exact opposite of the warrior she truly is.

Jeffrey's hand snakes around Lilith's waist. Every instinct in her body is probably to pommel him into the ground, but she resists. She instead swats at his hand with a high-pitched playful squeal, playing her role perfectly.

"Remove your hand from my wife before I remove it from your body," I growl.

Jeffrey chuckles while leaning back in his chair and removing his hand.

"You want to know what I think?" Jeffrey says, studying us. He's captured the room's attention.

Lilith is tense beside me as I grip her hand under the table, gently rubbing my thumb across her palm to keep her calm. It doesn't matter what he says. It doesn't matter, even if they know how skilled she is. All that matters is we are in this together.

"I think you're trying to fool us. I don't think you love her at all. I think she's here as a distraction. She's just some whore you can throw in our direction to distract us while you figure out how to win."

I yank Lilith out of her chair and pull her onto my lap.

"You don't think I love this woman?"

"No, I don't. I don't think you care if she lives or dies. You're nothing but her captor. You can play the chivalrous gentleman leader who fell in love with a woman, but you're no better than the rest of us. You're a monster. You brought her here to die because winning is that important to you."

I look directly into Jeffrey's brown eyes. I don't know what game he's playing or why he's calling us out. But I know he knows the truth. He knows exactly who Lilith is and what her skills are. *What game is he pulling? Why is he trying to convince the others?* I won't play along.

I grip Lilith's neck, hold her tightly to my body, and turn into the monster mob boss I'm supposed to be.

Lilith stiffens in my grasp, her heartbeat thundering against my chest.

"You're right. Lilith is mine. And what I do with her is my choice because she is my wife. Mine," I growl, staring down Jeffrey. "I don't care if you think I love her or not. I can do whatever the hell I want with her." My hands slide down her body, palming her breasts viciously, then sliding down her waist and gripping between her legs.

"Her body is mine. Her mind is mine. She does as I tell her. She does it because she's my wife. Because I love her. But also because she knows that as the leader of the Retribution Kings, I'm the most powerful man here. Stop messing with me before I kill you here and now."

Jeffrey's eyes thin into slits, looking from me to Lilith. "You're not the one I want."

All two dozen other eyes in the room look at Lilith with

a hunger that says we are totally fucked. My hand thrums against her stomach. We played this all wrong. We should have shown how skilled Lilith was from the start instead of hiding it.

Or better yet, the real Titus shouldn't have sent Lilith on this mission in the first place, knowing every man here would want to be the one to claim her and then kill her.

Our phones start buzzing, most likely telling us about the next round's challenge. No matter what the text says, I already know my mission.

If I were you, I'd walk out of this room right now because none of you are going to survive the next round. I'm going to kill you all.

CHAPTER 25

Lilith

I'M TAKING *the strongest member of your team. You have twenty-four hours to locate and retrieve them. Find them fast, for they will be tortured every hour they are taken. Failure to rescue your partner within twenty-four hours will result in their immediate execution.*

I read the text message, my eyes bulging at Hayes. We are about to be separated again. He's about to be taken, and I'll have the other competitors trying to kill me. It doesn't matter now that they know the truth of my skills; they're about to find out. It's the only way I'll be able to get Hayes back.

Hayes stares at me with as panicked an expression on his face as mine.

"I'll get you as fast as I can. I promise. I won't let The Abyss kill you. I won't let any of them kill you," he says.

I frown, confused by the words leaving his mouth. "No, I promise I'll save you—"

The sentence catches in my throat as the lights flash off. I reach out, finding Hayes's hand in the darkness as he finds mine as well. We both pull out our weapons—him a gun, me a knife. They can take one of us, but we aren't going to make it easy. I just got him back. I can't be separated from him, not again.

My heart thunders in my chest as quiet anticipation races through the room. The silent room waits. And waits. And waits. If anyone has been taken, it's been a silent snatching, which seems highly unlikely with this group.

Hayes's grip on my hand tightens, and I hear his whisper in the darkness. "I love you, Lily."

Are the words for the others? To remind them that the great Titus, leader of the Retribution Kings, loves me? To signal that I'm here as a supportive lover and not a threat?

Or are his words real?

"I lov—"

A needle is injected into my neck, and fog consumes my mind in the blink of an eye. I don't even have time to scream. The only thing left I can do is grip Hayes's hand with all of my might. I can't speak. I can't see. Even my breathing has slowed. My muscles quickly atrophy, growing weaker and weaker.

Hold on, hold on.

I do, far longer than should be possible. I feel Hayes with me until the last possible second when I'm ripped away.

———

My eyes open, but darkness still consumes my view. There's a pounding in my head, but somehow, I sense that I'm alone wherever I am.

"Titus," I whisper anyway, continuing our act in case anyone is listening. I'm not sure if I'm hoping Hayes is here or elsewhere. There's a part of me that hopes he's always here with me, even if it means we'll both die.

I try to stand up, only to find my arms shackled to the

wall above my head. Cold brick grits against my back. Dirt shifts under my legs. I'd guess I'm in some deranged man's basement. I look to my left and right but don't find any others here. It doesn't mean they aren't here, just that I can't see or sense them.

Still, I don't understand why I'm here instead of Hayes. *Wouldn't The Abyss consider Titus the stronger of us?*

"I know what you're thinking, and you're a fool to ask it," a deep mechanical voice says as if from a speaker.

I still and look up, but I don't see anyone here. *How could anyone rightly guess what I'm thinking?*

"You're far stronger than Titus, but maybe I chose wrongly if you think so little of yourself."

The Abyss—he's here. That must mean we are all here, at least in the same building. I wasn't expecting the man in charge to be involved in the games, but it seems he is. Although, he's hiding his voice to keep his identity a secret.

"You did choose wrong," I say. Hayes is far stronger than me in every way. He's smarter, kinder, stronger, funnier...

Fuck.

I love him.

I fell for him again. I've forgotten all the shit that he's done, all the damage he's caused me and my family.

There has to be a reason for Hayes's actions against my family. I can't reconcile the man I know with the man I thought he was, and I'm tired of trying. I'm tired of pretending I don't love him. I'm tired of pretending I don't wish I could have chosen him over Titus. And I can't believe that this is the fucking moment the realization hits me.

"No, I chose correctly. But for your sake, let's hope he's as strong and smart as you believe him to be. I'd hate to break your pretty little neck."

"He'll come for me," I snap back. Hayes will come for me long before the time is up.

"I'm sure he will, but it won't be soon enough to deny you any pain. The first hour is already up." A chime goes off, and the red glow of an alarm clock illuminates the table on which it sits across from me. It's the only thing I can make out in the room.

I heave a deep breath as the alarm stops, and the clank of a heavy door opening fills the space. The darkness of the room makes it hard for me to make out who is entering. Whoever they are, they don't speak. Suddenly, I feel two sets of hands undoing the metal shackles holding my wrists to the wall. When they release me, they don't give me any commands. They yank me to my feet, gripping my arms at the biceps and wrists so tightly that I'm afraid they'll break my arms if I make a single wrong move.

I should try to escape. This is my chance, I know that. But as I take my first step, the room spins. Whatever drugs they injected me with haven't fully left my system yet. There is no way I'm strong enough to run for it.

Instead, I'll have to observe everything I can and make a plan to get out while they torture me. I have every faith in Hayes rescuing me, but if I can make his job easier, I'm going to.

The men don't lead me far. Light streaks across my face from bright overhead bulbs as they march me into a large room with several doors along the walls.

It takes me several seconds of blinking to adjust to the brightness. I make out the other kidnapped competitors being marched into this room as well. The doors must each lead to an individual prison cell.

I don't have to ask what our torture will be when I see the twelve posts in the room. I force myself to take in the men holding onto my arms and memorize every one of their features. *What weapons do they carry? Do they have any limps or weaknesses? How many guards are there? There are two men to each competitor.*

I look for any differences in the doors, trying to identify which lead to other prisons and which might lead to an exit. I study everything I can as my arms are yanked in front of my body, and new shackles go around my wrists, tying me to the post.

Hands at the back of my shirt rip my shirt open, cool air flooding my back. Time slows as the chains are yanked tightly to the post, and my chest and face smash up against the wood. The rest of the room disappears from my vision, and all I see are my wrists bound in shackles.

I know what happens next, and yet, I really don't. I've endured a lot of suffering, a lot of emotional pain. I've let other men sexualize me and almost let other men fuck me all for the sake of getting revenge. But I've never suffered physical pain like I'm about to suffer.

The seconds tick by slowly, and my heart races in anticipation.

"You will be whipped for five minutes. When the time is up, you'll be brought back to your prison cell. If your teammates haven't rescued you when the next hour passes, then you'll be brought back out to be whipped for another five minutes. This will continue until you are rescued, or the sweet release of death comes for you in twenty-four hours," the same voice from my prison cell says over a loudspeaker, their voice still obscured.

Chills race down my spine. It's just a whipping. Only five minutes. Only twenty-four times. I get an hour's break each time. I can survive anything for five minutes.

"Begin," the voice says.

As soon as the word is spoken, my back receives a hard lash. My entire body jolts against the post, but there is nowhere to go. Tears sting in my eyes at the first crack. It already feels like my back has been split open.

The second whip hits my back nearly immediately, leaving me no time to catch my breath. My back arches as if that will somehow relieve me of the pain. Tears begin to fall down my face; I can't stop them.

But I bite down and clench my teeth together, refusing to cry out. I will not make a sound. I will not let them realize the extent of my suffering. I will not show weakness.

My head is dizzy by the third strike. By the fifth, I think, I lose all sense of time. *Have they been hitting me every second? How many strikes can they possibly give in five minutes?*

Others shout out in loud screams, whimpers, and cries of pain, echoing around the room. I shut them all out and focus on the only thought that will get me through this —Hayes.

I have to endure this. I don't have a choice. I need to tell Hayes how I feel. I need to tell him I love him. That I want him, despite everything. Despite what he did. Despite who I'm married to. Despite what we both still have to do. I know that I love him. I know there's a reason he's behaving the way he is, because I know he loves me too.

I'll get you, as fast as I can. I promise. I won't let The Abyss kill you. I won't let any of them kill you.

Hayes is coming. I'm the strong one. The Abyss chose me because I'm the strongest. So I'll be strong enough until Hayes comes.

CHAPTER 26

Hayes

NAUSEA SWIRLS in my gut as I blink my eyes open. A pounding headache greets me, as does the sound of others stirring. Although it's still dark, I know I'm still in the restaurant, and Lilith is gone.

The last thing I remember is tightly gripping her hand and whispering the words I should never say to her. Those words are only going to cause her more pain, and that's the last thing I want to do. Still, those words have never been more true.

I spring to my feet, unsure how long I've been out but remembering every word of the message. The Abyss was going to take the strongest—clearly, that was Lilith. They're going to torture her every hour until I rescue her.

Every second matters. Every second I don't go to her is a second she's going to be suffering in pain. And if I don't get to her in twenty-four hours, they'll kill her.

Not fucking happening.

I swallow, pushing down any remaining symptoms from the drugs they injected me with to kidnap Lilith.

For a split second, I hesitate. I look around the room at

the groggy men all half out of it. These men want to claim Lilith—rape her, torture her, kill her. Here and now, I have the opportunity to end them all.

But every second I waste, Lilith is suffering. I will not waste a single second on these bastards. I'll hold my promise and kill them later if any of them survive.

I pull my phone out of my pocket as I jog out of the restaurant. I make it to the elevator, step on, and press the button for ground before anyone else can get on.

I stare down at my phone as my stomach sours.

It's been one hour since Lilith was taken. I'm already too late to stop her from suffering any pain. She's being tortured right now, and there is nothing I can do to stop it.

I grind my teeth together as my hand fists at my side. The elevator doors open, and I step out, dialing the number simultaneously.

Gage answers on the first ring.

"Where's Lilith?" I ask.

"I assume she is with you," Gage snaps back.

"Lilith was kidnapped by The Abyss as part of the second round of the games from the Carbone restaurant. My job is to find her within twenty-four hours, or she dies. I only have twenty-three left, and she's being tortured every hour on the hour until she's rescued. Help me find her."

"I'll see what I can do, pulling up some security cameras. But if this was planned, I don't expect to find much. Anything I could find is probably a trap."

"Find her. We have to get her before the next hour is up." My mind spins with unimaginable pain that Lilith must be suffering right now. I won't let her suffer any longer than she has to.

"Gage," my voice breaks. "Tell me something, somewhere to start looking. I can't just stand out here on the street while Lilith is suffering."

"Search for any signs of security cameras on the surrounding streets, especially ones that The Abyss might not have been able to control."

"That's not good enough," I growl.

"It will have to be. I'm not a magician. I can't just pull footage out of my ass. This is going to take some time. All you can do is look for cameras or search surrounding buildings where you think she might be held. If you're lucky, you'll find someone who saw something that you can question."

"The waiter staff. They have to have seen something."

I rush back into the restaurant, hoping for a fucking miracle. But after questioning everyone over the course of an hour, I'm no better off than I was before.

Gage still doesn't have any answers for me, and panic starts to set in—only twenty-two hours left. I can't keep letting her suffer. I have to find her, now. Before The Abyss takes more from her. Before she loses another part of herself to the pain and suffering she's enduring.

I go through my options. Tracking the others to see if they have figured out where The Abyss took them. The security cameras. Looking into anything we know about The Abyss and where their bases of operation might be.

I stare at my phone, knowing what I need to do. I have to do everything to rescue her, no matter the cost.

I dial Titus's number. "I need your help. It's about Lilith."

CHAPTER 27

Lilith

THE ALARM GOES off in the darkness. It used to jolt me into flight or fight mode—set my adrenaline coursing through my body. But now, after so many times, my body barely registers the sound. I don't move. I don't so much as open my eyes as the now familiar hands grab onto my body, undo the iron at my wrists, and drag me into the brightly lit room to my whipping post.

At this point, I'm not even sure why they bother to restrain me. I don't have the strength to lift my own head, let alone fight or run. I'm completely at their mercy.

There is one thing I have kept track of, though—one part of my brain that still works. I know exactly how many times that alarm has gone off. How many times I've been dragged out here and tied to this post. How many times I've been whipped to within an inch of death.

Twenty-three.

This is the twenty-third time.

I force my eyes open for a split second, just long enough to gaze quickly around the room before the first lash hits my skin. Everyone is still here; no one has been rescued. By the look of some of the other contestants, I'm not sure how many of them are actually still alive.

I don't bother bracing myself for the first lash of the whip. There is no use. It won't save me from the pain. It won't save my back from splitting open. It won't keep me alive.

The whip strikes my back, and my body seizes. I thought by this point, any nerve endings on my back would be numb, but I feel every impact as painfully as the first one.

My arms burn as they hold up the weight of my body. I'm so tired. I just want to sleep. My eyes drift closed between each whip, giving me micro naps, but it's not enough.

My breathing is slow and ragged. Blood barely seems to be moving through my body anymore. I don't know how much longer I can hold out.

Twenty-three. This is number twenty-three. Time is almost up.

Hayes will save me. I know it. I have complete faith in him. He'll save me.

But if he doesn't, if he can't, this all ends in one more hour. In one more hour, the pain goes away no matter if he comes or not.

I smile at the thought of that, of no more pain. And then my mind drifts to where it always does, making my grin even wider.

His long hair falling out of the bun on top of his head. His sharp eyes smirking at me beneath his sexy glasses. His grin smiling up at me between the shadows of the scruff on his unshaven face.

I think of his thick muscles wrapping around my body, shielding me, protecting me, keeping me safe. And then my mind drifts to all the dirty things I want to do with him, to the last time we were together.

He assumed it was a mistake, but it wasn't. It was the best decision of my life. Loving him has never been a mistake. He's a man worth loving, even if he's hidden several truths from me. Even though he's lied to me. I know it's all because he loves me too.

Hayes loves me.

And I love him.

That love will survive this.

We will survive this.

Hayes comes into my vision even more clearly than before. I must have finally fallen asleep and be dreaming to see him so clearly.

"You're safe, Lilith. You're safe."

CHAPTER 28

Lilith

"EASY, BABY," a man's voice sounds in my head as my eyes flitter open. When I open my eyes, the man next to my bed isn't the man I want to see.

Titus smiles gently at me, his hand stroking my hair. There's a hint of concern he can't keep out of his eyes.

"Easy," he says again as I try to sit up more.

"I'm fine," I say, needing to look around the room, needing to see Hayes.

"You're not fine. You've been out for three days, and you're on a high doses of narcotics to keep the pain and inflammation down."

Three days.

It's been three whole days.

I blink as I take in the words and remember what happened. How my back must look. But he's right; I don't feel any pain.

I stare down at the tube leading into my hand and hooked up to a fluid bag hanging on a pole to my left. As I quickly look around the room, I realize I'm not in a hospital.

"We're in a penthouse hotel suite. A doctor comes to

181

visit you three times a day. After the last check, they said your back is healing nicely, and other than the pain and some scars, you should recover well."

I nod as he shares the news, unsure of how to ask my next question. But before I can, Titus breaks down in tears. "I'm so sorry."

I narrow my eyes, not processing his emotion.

"I'm so sorry, baby. I should have never asked you to do this. I should have done it myself without you or at least entered the game with you. I shouldn't have risked your life like this. I'm so sorry. I'll find a way to get you out of the competition."

I shake my head. "No."

He stops stroking my hair and cocks his head. "Lilith, I'm not risking your life. You've suffered enough."

"And I want to finish what I started. Otherwise, it's all for nothing."

"Lilith—"

"I'm doing this. Stop trying to convince me otherwise."

Titus bites his lip but doesn't push it any further. But I can see the raw emotion on his face and know we'll be revisiting this conversation soon.

"Speaking of the competition, have there been any messages?"

"No, nothing. But after how severely you were injured, I'd expect The Abyss to wait a few days before continuing. Competitors unable to even lift their own heads wouldn't make for a very entertaining final round for them."

I nod, agreeing. *How much time will they actually give us? How much time do I actually want?*

"And Hayes?" I ask, trying to keep the emotion from my voice.

"He was able to rescue you, thank god. But not until the

very last minute," Titus says, a bit of anger dripping in his voice.

I frown at his reaction. Hayes did his best to rescue me. He didn't purposefully wait until the last second.

"And where were you?" I snap.

"I was traveling here as fast as I could the second Hayes called me. But I'm sorry it wasn't fast enough."

Titus sounds sincere.

"I want to talk to Hayes. I want to learn what happened."

"Later," Titus says.

I frown, not understanding why I can't talk to Hayes now. But I let it go as I yawn and realize my exhaustion is going to take hold of me again.

"You should rest. You're safe here. I'll be right here by your side as much as I can. Gage has a full team here guarding the hotel suite. You're safe. No one is going to hurt you here."

I nod, but my eyes have already drifted shut, the pull of sleep too strong to keep them open a second longer.

———

The next time I wake up, I find the room empty and the IV still in my hand. My back is still completely numb, so the amount of drugs pumping through me are still extensive.

A second later, the door flies open, and my heart races.

"Ha—" I start but realize it's Gage entering the room.

"I'm sorry, Titus had to take a meeting, so he stepped out for a few minutes. He's been at your side all night, though."

"I'm sure he has," I say with a sigh.

"Can I get you anything? Are you hungry? Bored? I can bring you a book. Here's the TV remote," Gage says.

"I could eat," I reply, putting the remote on the night-stand next to me.

"What sounds good? I can get you anything."

"Will Hayes be the one cooking for me?" I ask.

Gage stills. "No."

"Where is he? Why hasn't he come to see me?"

"He's just giving you and Titus some privacy."

I frown. "Tell Hayes I don't need privacy. I need to talk to him."

Gage nods and quickly walks out the door.

This pattern continues on and on for about a week. Titus fawns over me, treating me like a fragile princess. Gage mostly avoids me except when he can't because Titus has to work. Gage promises me that he's talked to Hayes.

And yet, Hayes never comes.

"Remove the IV," I say to Titus the evening my patience has run out.

"But it's the best way to handle your pain."

I shake my head. "I can handle the pain. I'm tired of having a tube in my arm. Take it out, or I will."

Titus sighs, but within a half-hour, a doctor is removing my IV and explaining oral pain meds.

"Thank you," I tell Titus when the doctor has left.

"I just don't want to see you in pain."

"I know." But I'm tired of feeling nothing.

My phone buzzes on my nightstand as if The Abyss knows I've healed enough.

We both glance over at the phone. My heart races, and I pick up the phone before Titus can grab it.

The competition will continue in one week.

There's no information about the next challenge, but I have one week to finish healing. To get back into shape. To figure out how I'm going to win this game.

But more importantly, I have one week to rescue Hayes.

Titus reads the message over my shoulder. "Lilith, please don't—"

"I'm doing this. I need to do this. Please, don't try to stop me. Help me instead."

Titus nods. "Anything, I'll do anything. I just wish I could finish the game with you."

"But you can't."

Titus frowns and opens his mouth to argue more but stops himself.

"We need to sleep. Tomorrow, I need to get back to training."

Titus sighs but nods.

I climb out of bed to go to the bathroom, but Titus quickly grabs my elbow, trying to help me.

"I've got it."

"I know, but I—"

I shake my head. "I need to do this. All of it, myself."

He sighs. "I just care about you and don't want you to suffer."

"I know. I care about you, too. But I don't need to be coddled."

He nods but follows me to the bathroom anyway.

"I'm just getting ready for bed. I wouldn't dare help you." He grins as he begins to brush his teeth.

I eye him carefully, but he sticks to his word, and I get ready for the first time in a week without anyone's help. Titus finishes first and heads back to the bedroom, while I finish washing my face.

Then, the aching starts—dull and throbbing.

I haven't dared to look at my back, at how it's healing or the scars I'm sure are already forming. I try not to think about what I went through. If I let myself go back to that place, I'll never escape again.

I walk back to the bedroom with the ache growing heavier. But I refuse to take the medication on the nightstand. I need to get used to this pain. I need full use of my body to survive and win the final round.

When I walk back into the bedroom, I find a shirtless Titus already in bed.

I rake my eyes over his naked torso.

"Don't look at me like that. I don't have any self-control when it comes to you," he says.

But I'm not looking at him in the way he thinks. I'm looking at him because the man I really want isn't here. And even though they are so different, Titus reminds me of Hayes.

I climb into bed and roll over onto my side to keep from causing more pain to my back. Then I pretend to sleep, waiting for Titus to finally drift off.

When I hear the gentle roll of his snores, I climb out of bed. The ache in my back is barely noticeable as I focus on my mission.

The penthouse suite is quiet as I walk out of the bedroom. There are guards in the hallway, though. I'm sure they've spotted me by now on the cameras they likely have in the common rooms.

It doesn't surprise me when Gage appears a minute after I step out of the bedroom.

"Where is he?" I say quietly.

Gage sighs and stares at me. For a moment, I don't think he's going to answer me, but then he does.

"Follow me."

My heart thunders as I follow Gage out to a hallway with three other doors. He motions to the last door on the right. He looks at me with a steady, tortured gaze. He wants to tell me something; he's fighting with himself over whether he should tell me or not. But ultimately, he says nothing.

I open the door but keep my eyes on Gage to look for

any last-second clue as to what I'm going to find when I enter the room. But he offers me nothing.

I turn, expecting to find a sleeping Hayes, but what I find shocks me.

Hayes is standing shirtless in the bathroom, his back to me. His gaze stares back at me in the mirror before I get a good look at his back. His back is completely shattered and torn up.

I gasp, and tears fall instantly.

"What happened?" I whisper, needing to know everything, needing to know what this man went through to save me.

CHAPTER 29

Hayes

I'M NOT sure if Lilith is actually standing in my doorway or if it's an angel from my dreams. It's been a week since I've seen her. I wasn't sure how I was going to feel when we saw each other again, but the sight of her takes my breath away. She's more beautiful than in my dreams.

I want to run to her, scoop her up in my arms, and inspect every inch of her. But I don't move from the bathroom counter.

Her eyes scan over every inch of angry red split-open skin on my back. My skin tells her exactly what happened when I saved her.

The sharp gasp that leaves her mouth pulls at my heart. The tears falling hurt worse.

I've been avoiding her until my back was healed, because I didn't want her to know what happened to me. I didn't want her to carry the burden of me suffering in order to save her.

The added bonus of staying away was giving her and Titus some time together. Maybe he could convince her to drop out of the competition.

"What happened?" Her voice breaks as she speaks.

I walk back into the bedroom and pull a shirt over my head, while doing everything I can to hold back the pain I'm in. I haven't been wearing a shirt most days, but I don't want her to keep staring at my back and thinking about the pain I must be in.

"When I finally found where you were kept, they wouldn't let me take you away until I suffered everything I forced you to endure. I had to endure twenty-three five-minute lashings—the same amount of pain you went through. Only then did they release us both."

"That looks like they tortured you far more than me," she says quietly, tears still in her eyes.

I frown. "Have you looked at what your own back?"

She shakes her head slowly.

I take a deep breath. "You should see."

She takes my outstretched hand, and together, we walk to the bathroom. Her breathing is ragged as she stands with her back to the mirror.

"I'm right here."

"I know," she says with a soft smile. She releases my hand and lifts her shirt over her head. I hand her a small mirror from a bathroom drawer so she can see.

Seeing her suffering etched into her skin, she sucks in a sharp breath. She studies every red strike, broken piece of skin, and stitch holding her back together.

It doesn't look as bad as when I first found her, but...I choke back a sob. "I'm so sorry, Lily. I'm sorry I didn't get to you sooner. I'm sorry you had to endure that for so long. I'm so fucking sorry."

Her head snaps to me, confusion plastered on her face.

"When you came to rescue me, you saw me? You knew what you'd have to endure in order to rescue me?"

I nod.

"You could have just let me die. You didn't have to suffer this."

I frown, grabbing her face and looking deep into her eyes. "There was no way I was going to let you die. I promised I'd rescue you, no matter what."

"I knew you were going to rescue me. There was never a doubt in my mind."

My shoulders slump slightly in relief. "I was so afraid that you'd give up hope of me rescuing you with every hour that passed."

"Never."

I blink back my tears as I release her face and force myself to take a step back from her, ignoring her bare naked chest.

"I don't regret the pain I endured," she says.

"What?"

"I don't regret it because it was in those moments that my mind finally became clear. I finally realized the truth."

I realize where she's going with this, and I can't let her say it.

"Lilith, I—"

"I love you, Hayes. I've always loved you. I loved you before I knew the truth. I loved you even when you lied to me. And I still love you."

I still, unable to respond to her declaration.

"And I forgive you. Not for taking as long as you did to rescue me; you don't need my forgiveness for that. I know you rescued me as quickly as you can, and I'm so very thankful and furious for what you had to go through to save me. I forgive you for everything else. For lying to me. For killing my father. All of it."

Fuck me. I've wanted to hear those words for so long, and they still destroy me. I can't possibly respond to her because I don't deserve her love. *How can she forgive me when I haven't told her the truth? How can she love me?*

She doesn't wait for me to respond. She kisses me, capturing my lips with a single kiss. I can't possibly deny her. I can't possibly stop this. There is no force in the world great enough to stop what's between us, especially not now that she loves me and is openly admitting it.

I want to wrap my arms around her body and hold her close to me, never letting her go. But I resist, not wanting to hurt her. Instead, I gently caress the back of her head as I kiss her.

She growls against my lips as her hands begin to lift the hem of my shirt up, her hands cool against my warm skin. She isn't reserved or cautious at all. Her touch is aggressive and needy and begging—begging me for something that she's not sure I'm willing to give up.

She doesn't know the truth. I would give her anything— the whole world. But I would do more to keep her safe, and I'm not safe.

Her hands yank my shirt over my head until our chests are skin-to-skin.

"Stop it. Stop holding back," she purrs.

My eyes search hers as I barely stroke her hair. "I don't want to hurt you."

"You never could."

I shake my head. "I think you must have gotten a concussion or something if you believe that."

She chuckles but then pulls my bottom lip into her mouth, sucking hard.

I groan.

Her eyes alight with desire. Her fire forces me to finally give her what she's begging me for—all of me.

I kiss her with everything I have, not worrying about tomorrow, just this moment right now. My hands grip her ass as I lift her onto the counter in the bathroom. Her hands tangle in my hair, pulling me in between her legs.

"I need you inside me, now," she purrs against my lips.

I grin, already a step ahead of her, as I push down my pajama pants and boxer briefs.

She smiles back with hooded eyes as I grab her waistband, and she lifts her hips for me to yank them off of her.

I suck in a harsh breath at the sight of her.

"You're so beautiful," I crack out.

She tilts her head. "I'm yours."

I swallow down that truth as I settle back between her legs. As I do, I spot her back in the mirror and tense. She'll carry those marks for the rest of her life. She'll always remember the trauma that I couldn't save her from—a trauma we share.

I kiss down her neck and over the curve of her breast, wishing I could kiss every piece of her flesh until all she thinks about is my kisses instead of the pain I know still wrecks her body. But I know her back is still far too tender to be kissed yet.

I take her nipple into my mouth as I kneel in front of her. Her hands grip the counter as she arches her back, giving into the pleasure.

I take my time with both of her nipples, sweeping my tongue across them until they are hard against my touch, and I can smell her arousal pooling between her legs. Only then do I sink lower, kissing down her smooth stomach. I spread her legs and sweep my tongue between her folds, licking over her clit.

She shudders and curses as a small orgasm pulses through her, and her arousal floods over my tongue.

"Fuck me, Hayes. Please."

I can't hold back any longer. I'm standing and inside her in one quick thrust. Our bodies mold together as I fuck her on the counter in the bathroom. With every thrust, the image of her back gets more ingrained in my memory. The need to ease her pain intensifies. And words that are harder and harder to bite back consume my thoughts.

Mine.

I love you.

Mine.

A knock on my door has me pausing mid-thrust.

"Lilith?" I hear Titus say through the door.

Fuck.

My heart stammers as I look at Lilith. Titus is going to kill me for fucking his wife. But I won't let him punish Lilith. She's endured enough.

My mind whirls with thoughts of how I can make Titus believe that I'm fucking Lilith against her will. But Lilith places a hand on my chest with a wicked gleam in her eyes.

I shake my head, but Lilith grabs my hair and pulls me toward her.

"Don't you dare," she whispers against my lips before kissing me hard.

My body automatically starts fucking her again, my brain no longer working.

"Yes," she moans.

I thrust harder, my thumb reaching between us to rub her clit.

"I'm so close," she moans again.

In the back of my brain, I hear another knock, but I tune it out. I can't stop. I can't do anything but fuck her and bring her pleasure.

"Hayes!" she cries out as an orgasm rips through her. She's usually loud when she orgasms, but this cry is different. It's louder than any before, almost as if she's doing it on purpose. As if she wants Titus to hear her.

I try to hold back, to be quiet, but when I pour my orgasm into her, I cry out her name as loudly as she did mine. I don't care about the consequences. I don't care that

Titus definitely heard us. I don't care if it's the last thing I do before I die.

I expect Titus to come barreling through the door, but the hallway is quiet as I lift Lilith off the counter.

I carry her to my bed and kiss her swollen lips gently as I lie her down on my bed. I climb into the bed next to her and run my hand through her hair. We stare at each other, but her eyes quickly grow heavy.

"I love you, Hayes," she whispers as her eyes fall shut.

I watch her as she sleeps in my bed. Tonight feels like a goodbye. I'm hoping that's only because of what Titus is going to do to me and not because I'm going to lose her in the final round of the game.

I wait until she's fast asleep, until her soft snores fill the room. "I love you, too, Lily."

CHAPTER 30

Lilith

THE REST OF THE WEEK, I only see Hayes during training. We don't talk about what happened that night. We don't share any more intimate moments. We are completely focused on getting back into the best shape of our lives so we can survive the final game.

Titus doesn't confront either of us about what happened that night either. He definitely heard us, and he definitely noticed that I never returned to his bed that night.

We are all so focused on training and surviving and winning that nothing else matters. I know Titus doesn't care who I fuck as long as I do it discreetly. The only thing he cares about is his reputation with the Retribution Kings.

At least, I don't think he cares until the final day before the game. Titus challenged Hayes to a fight, claiming he wanted to make sure Hayes was ready to protect me in the game. But I'd never seen rage like I saw on Titus's face when they fought. I've always thought Hayes was the better fighter, but Titus kicked Hayes's ass. And he promised more ass-kicking if anything happened to me today.

Gage parks the car the four of us are riding in to the final challenge.

"Give us a minute," Titus says from the back seat he's sharing with me.

Gage just nods and steps out, but Hayes glances back at me for permission. I nod subtly, and Hayes reluctantly steps out of the car.

"I'm sorry," I say before Titus says anything. "I'm sorry I wasn't loyal to you."

Titus looks at me with steel in his eyes. "Win the game. And then come back to me, Lilith." He leans over and kisses me in a claiming kiss.

I blink, shocked by his kiss and words.

"Come back to me, or I'll never stop searching for you."

I swallow but nod once.

Then we both step out of the car, and Hayes settles in next to me, taking my hand in his. Titus glares at our joined hands for a second.

"Just playing the part. From this moment forward, I'm Titus, and you're Hayes," Hayes says to Titus.

Titus shakes off his glare and grins a little too widely as we step into the building. We walk to the elevator, and Gage presses the button for the basement as I bask in the feeling of holding Hayes's hand again.

The doors open, and Hayes gently squeezes my hand.

I squeeze right back. We're in this together. The two of us. Not Titus and me. Not Gage and us. Just the two of us. They can't help us now.

Titus and Gage step out first, followed by Hayes and I. I thought I'd be an anxious wreck after what happened last time, but my heartbeat is calm and steady. As long as Hayes and I aren't separated again, we'll win.

As we step foot into the basement, I'm surprised to see a large crowd gathered. I have no idea who all these people are. *Do they work for The Abyss? Are they members of other gangs?*

Hayes and I exchange a nervous glance but don't speak otherwise.

The crowd is standing in a circle around two fighting rings.

I grin. Finally, we get to battle it out with the remaining competitors. We are more than ready.

I squeeze Hayes's hand again. He squeezes right back. *We've got this.*

The robotic voice sounds through the room's speakers, silencing everyone. "Will the competitors Jeffrey and Michael step into the first ring?"

Hayes and I both exhale in relief as we see them walk in. They are on the same team, which means Hayes and I will get to fight the other competitors together. This is even better.

"Will competitors Titus and Lilith step into the second ring?"

Hayes and I step forward in our all-black gear. We are armed and ready for this fight. Hayes helps me up into the ring before climbing up himself.

We stare out at the crowd, waiting to see who we will face. I'm not surprised that Jeffrey and his teammate Michael survived the last round, but I don't know who else did.

"You four are our finalists," the voice says, and my heart jumps in my throat.

I reach over for Hayes's hand again, needing him close as the ominous voice echoes through the room again.

"But there can only be one winner," the voice continues.

My heart slams to a stop as I squeeze Hayes's hand so tightly that I know he's not getting blood to his fingertips anymore.

"First, you will battle your teammate...to the death."

I close my eyes, not believing the words.

"You must prove your loyalty to me. If you want to be my ally, you will put me above everyone else. Once you kill your teammate, then you will meet your final competitor in the ring. The last one standing wins the honor of being my most trusted ally. My second, if you will. And I'll owe you a debt."

Tears stain my eyelids, but I hold them back. Hayes doesn't let go of my hand.

I don't know how we are going to survive this. *How are we supposed to fight each other? Kill each other?*

There was a time when that would have been easy, a time when I hated Hayes for what he did. But that time has long passed.

"Begin," the voice says, and the room cheers.

I open my eyes and look around to realize the crowd is loyal to The Abyss. They work for him. He must be somewhere in this room. He wouldn't miss this, *but where is he?*

"Do it," Hayes says, releasing my hand.

"What?"

"Do it. Kill me."

I frown. "No."

"You've wanted to for a long time, and I deserve it."

I stare into his eyes, into the eyes of the man I love. This man is willing to sacrifice his life for me—he has always been willing to.

"I'm a dead man anyway. You know Titus will kill me for what I did," Hayes says in a whisper so only I can hear him.

I frown. "No."

He runs at me in an attack, forcing me to block him, to fight back. I block him, but that's it. I refuse to do more than our normal sparring. I don't draw a weapon, nothing.

But Hayes doesn't hold back. He comes at me hard,

attacking again and again, until my moves become automatic.

We fight like we have a hundred times, throwing punches and kicks and blocks. But neither of reach for our weapons.

A gunshot is fired, drawing my attention away from Hayes. Michael is lying in a pool of blood at Jeffrey's feet.

I won't let that be Hayes.

"I killed your father in cold blood; that's why I never told you. He knew my secrets. He was a threat to me, so I killed him."

"No," I whisper, throwing a punch that connects with Hayes's jaw. He falls hard to the ground.

"I killed your sisters. I killed your friend."

My heart stops. *Oh, Hayes, my dear sweet Hayes.*

He'll do anything to save me, even claim to have done something I know he didn't. They're all alive, enjoying traveling through Europe.

But I'll do anything to save him, too—anything.

I pull out a dagger and clench my teeth, letting the rage of our situation flow through me. Pointing my dagger at him, I don't let him realize that I intend to slit my own throat rather than drive it into his heart.

Suddenly, a different solution shines in the crowd. It's a long shot, and we'll probably both end up dead. But if it gives us both a one percent chance to live, then that's a chance I'm willing to take. I fling the dagger into the crowd, jump out of the ring, and chase after the person my dagger found.

CHAPTER 31

Lilith

I DON'T KNOW how I knew it was them when I flung the dagger into the crowd. Just a strong, overwhelming feeling. They watched us carefully, in a more calculated way than everyone else who just cared about how bloody and entertaining the fights were.

I run as fast I can after The Abyss, but they're fast, even with a dagger stuck in their chest. But they are alone. No guards surround them or follow us as we run for the stairs.

The Abyss has a head start up the stairs, but I'm right on their heels.

They only run up one flight of stairs and dart through the lobby of the building. They run toward the first door.

Glancing behind me, I expect a trove of people to be following us, but there are still none.

The Abyss opens a door, and I follow, a dagger drawn. As the door falls shut behind me, I'm prepared to end all of this.

"Well done, Lilith. I always had faith in you."

I freeze. "What?"

"I declare you the winner."

"Only because I'm about to put a dagger in your heart if you don't."

The Abyss smirks in the darkness of what appears to be an office. The lights are off, so it's hard to make out their features. But their smirk becomes clear as my eyes begin to adjust to the darkness, and more of their features come to light.

"If you wanted me dead, I'd already be. You entered the game for a reason, and that reason wasn't to kill me."

"That was before you tried to force me to kill the man I love."

The Abyss steps forward, and I can see her clearly now. She's a striking woman with bleach-blonde hair, full lips, and very feminine features. She's the complete opposite of who I expected to see when I met The Abyss.

"I'm sorry about that. Truly, I am. But I had to test you, and you passed with flying colors."

"But I didn't kill my partner," I say.

"Exactly. I don't want someone who is willing to kill their own people in order to win. I want someone loyal to be my ally."

I frown. "I still want to kill you for that."

"I know."

"And yet, you trust me?"

"More than I've ever trusted anyone." She prances over to behind the desk, sits in the large desk chair, and puts her feet up on the desk, completely at ease.

I continue to hold onto my dagger as I approach the desk she's sitting behind. I don't bother sitting. She may trust me, but I don't trust her. I'll be ready for any other trap or game she plans on playing.

"Now, ask me the questions you came here to ask me."

I narrow my eyes at her, watching her every move. "It would be nice to know who I'm talking to first. I prefer not to refer to you as The Abyss any longer."

"Nova. My name is Nova."

"What happened to the woman my husband loves, Nova?"

She hesitates for a second. "You're here for Iris."

"Yes."

"A fool's errand. Why risk everything on the chance that I know the whereabouts of the woman your husband loves? Unless you plan on killing her?"

"I love Hayes, not Titus."

Her lips curl up in a cruel grin.

"Ah, but does Hayes love you?"

"Yes."

"Has he told you that? Even if he has, Hayes is a great manipulator. The best, perhaps."

I frown. "You know Hayes?"

"I know all of the Retribution Kings. I know he's been parading around as Titus this entire time."

I grip my dagger harder in my hand. Nova doesn't so much as glance at the weapon I hold.

"You're sure he loves you?"

"Yes," I say flatly.

"Then, you don't want to find Iris. Finding her would be putting your love to the test."

"How so?"

"All of the Retribution Kings love Iris, every single one of them."

I don't care who does or does not love Iris. I care about the tense she uses. "So, Iris is alive?"

"That's the wrong question to ask," Nova says, seeming bored with this line of conversation.

"You owe me a debt. This is that debt. Tell me everything you know about Iris."

She sighs. "Such a boring way to repay a debt, but if you insist. The Retribution Kings have been chasing Iris for years, like she's some mythical goddess that has a hold of them. I don't understand it. Even when she died, they couldn't accept it. They believed she had to live."

"Who is they?"

"Lennox, Gage, Hayes, and Titus. Although, the others didn't realize that Titus knew her and was searching for her."

I still, not sure I want to hear this story. But I promised Titus. I know how much Titus loved Iris, how heartbroken he is. And now that I'm trapped in a marriage to him, the only way he might release me so that I can freely be with Hayes is if I find Iris for him.

"They were all her lovers. All of them. She loved them all."

I frown. It doesn't change the fact that Hayes loves me. It's the one thing I will never question again.

"But she couldn't have all of them forever. Eventually, she'd have to choose."

"She chose Titus?"

"No, she chose Lennox."

My eyebrows jump. I wasn't expecting that. "The leader of the Corsi mafia, who is currently married, and very much in love with his wife?"

She nods, her eyes distant. "The very same."

"Why did she choose him?"

"Because she was pregnant."

"With his child?"

"No, another's."

"Whose?"

Her eyes center back to me with a knowing look.

My heart stops. "Hayes."

"Yes, Iris was pregnant by the man you love. But she didn't think he would make a good father, so she told Lennox it was his instead."

"Did Hayes know the truth?"

"What do you think?" She smiles viciously, excited to watch my emotional suffering.

"Yes, Hayes knew the truth."

She nods. "But he was willing to lie to everyone. Lennox believed he was the father, and he mourned as a father when the child was viciously taken from them."

"In a freak accident?"

Her head snaps to me. "No, when the child was murdered."

I swallow back my tears. Hayes's child was murdered. He had a child he could never claim, and then that child was murdered. No wonder Hayes wants to die. The pain he endures on a daily basis must be immense.

I'm sure there's more that Nova knows, but I've heard enough.

"We are allies, you and I," she says.

"We'll see about that," I snap.

She shakes her head with a light laugh. "Definitely allies. If you need me, all you have to do is call, and I will assist you in any way I can. But I expect the same of you."

"Why? Why do all of this? Why have an ally? Did you do this to take out your enemies?"

"Perhaps. Or perhaps it's lonely with no one knowing who you are."

I frown. "The men who work for you—"

"They don't know who I am. I lead them all with smoke and mirrors. If they found out I was a woman, they'd try to kill me. I held the competition because I'm tired of constantly hiding. I need someone I can trust."

I see her pain then. This woman has been through incredible pain. I don't know her story. I don't know how she became The Abyss—the most ruthless crime lord in all of America.

But I realize now that I do trust her in the same way I trust Hayes. It's a gut feeling, something I feel deep in my soul. I should trust her, despite all the evidence to the contrary.

She hands me a piece of paper with a number on it. "Memorize it, and then destroy it. Call it if you need me."

After memorizing the number and shredding the paper, I stare at her intensely. "What is your name?"

She smiles. "You already know my name."

"You're Iris, aren't you?"

She pauses. "I was, but I'm not anymore. That chapter of my life has closed. I am Nova now."

I swallow my shock. She's alive. The woman they all think is dead is truly alive. And she's turned into a ruthless leader.

I turn to leave. I've heard enough for now. I need to hear the rest from Hayes.

"Tell them Iris is dead. They need to stop searching for her. She's gone."

I pause, looking at her one last time. "I can't make any promises."

"I know," she grins. "That's why I think you and I are going to become more than allies. You're as vicious as I am."

I can't help it. I smile back, my eyebrow curling up. "That we are. I'll be calling you very soon. There is someone who deserves to hear the truth from you."

I expect Nova to argue with me, to tell me there is no way she'll show her face to any of them. Instead, she nods. Maybe we will become friends after all.

"Hayes is waiting for you in a hotel suite at the Four Seasons."

I pause. "What? How do you—"

"I want to be allies and friends. This is my offering to show I truly mean that."

I don't thank her. I don't wait for another second. I just go.

CHAPTER 32

Hayes

NOT CHASING Lilith was incredibly hard, until I saw the flash of bleached-blonde hair Lilith was chasing after.

Go to the Four Seasons. There is a room booked in your name. Lilith will meet you there soon.

-I

'I'—I know exactly who The Abyss is. I know who is responsible for everything. My feelings for her are complicated. I loved her; I hated her. But she's alive, and Lilith is with her. I have no doubt that Lilith will learn everything Iris knows.

But I don't care. All I care is that Iris is alive. I don't know how she isn't dead or how she became The Abyss, but she's alive.

My heart floods at that thought. I can tell Lennox. Lennox deserves to know the woman he loved is alive. I don't know what he'll do with that information, since he now loves Rialta. And Iris threatened Rialta's life many times. His feelings for Iris will be even more complicated than my own. But at least his heart can rest easy knowing Iris survived. What he does after finding out is up to him.

That is until she tells him the truth.

He'll hate me for it, and he'll hate her too.

I don't know if it's better to keep that secret hidden, but at least it won't be a burden I have to bear alone.

I pace the hotel room, unsure of how long I'll have to wait. Iris won't hurt Lilith. No matter how Iris has changed in the time since I last saw her, she won't kill Lilith.

I don't know what Titus is going to do, though. He'll still probably try to kill me. I ran before he could catch up to me.

But now I wait for Lilith to arrive.

"I love you."

Her words make me jump. I don't know how she got into the hotel room without me realizing she was here. I turn, facing Lilith with tears in my eyes. I never thought I'd see her again. I thought I'd die tonight, but she found a way to save me.

I shake my head as I run to her and wrap my arms around her in a tight hug.

"If you still love me, then it means Iris didn't tell you everything."

She grips my shoulders, refusing to let me go as she looks me in the eyes. "Nova told me enough."

"Nova?"

"That's what she goes by now."

I frown.

"What did she tell you?"

She shakes her head and takes a deep breath, her head dropping down before she glances back up at my face. "Why did you kill my father?"

I bite my lip.

"Why did you kill my father?" she asks gently.

I shake my head, refusing to answer the question.

"Nova didn't tell me that part. I didn't want her to. I need to hear it from you. Why did you kill my father?"

I step back, and her arms drop from my shoulders. "I already told you. I was a killer."

"No, I don't believe you. Just like I didn't believe when you said you killed my sisters and friend, who are very much alive because me and Titus were the ones that faked their deaths." She takes a step toward me.

I take another step back, my heart soaring at the news that her sisters and friend are alive. But now isn't the time to discuss that.

"Your father knew my secret and was threatening to reveal it."

She shakes her head as she takes another step, and tears fill her eyes. "No, tell me the truth."

"The truth doesn't matter. The truth is I killed him. I killed your father. You can never forgive me. You should have killed me. It's the only thing that would take away your pain."

"You telling me the truth is the only thing that will take away my pain. I love you, Hayes. No matter the truth, I will always love you."

"You won't."

She glares. "You stubborn man. I love you. And I already know the truth in my heart. I just need you to confirm it."

"I'm not a good man."

"You are. You're the best man."

"I lie. I'm a whore. I cheat. I manipulate. I kill."

She takes a gentle step and reaches out, taking my hand in hers.

I squeeze my eyes shut at her touch, barely able to stand it.

"Please," she begs.

"I promised I wouldn't hurt you."

"This won't hurt me."

"It will."

She touches her hand to my cheek, and I open my eyes. "But *you* won't be the one that hurts me."

My eyes water, but I can't speak the truth.

"Tell me what my father did. Tell me what kind of a monster he was. Tell me the truth."

I suck in a breath; not sure how she realized it, but I don't have a choice. I tell her the words that will break her heart.

"Your father was one of the men who murdered my daughter."

A single tear rolls down Lilith's cheek, but she doesn't scream or cry in anguish. She doesn't close her eyes or back away from me. She doesn't deny my statement.

"I love you, Hayes," she repeats.

My heart breaks for her as I pull her tight to my body and hug her with everything I have.

"I'm so sorry, Lily. I'm so sorry."

"You have nothing to be sorry for. If my father was still alive, I'd kill him myself."

"I don't deserve you, Lilith."

"You don't," Lilith teases.

I grin through my tears, through the pain I never let myself feel.

"But you love me anyways," she says.

"I do—I love you, Lily."

Her lips collide with mine, and we kiss and kiss and kiss.

"I'm yours—forever," she says in between kisses.

Our hands intertwine, and I feel the ring on her finger. We both stop, our wildest fantasies about what our future could bring already coming crashing to a halt.

"Except I'm already married," she says.

"Fuck. Titus is never going to let you go." My mind starts swirling.

"Titus loved Iris, too. He was one of her lovers."

My heart halts. "He chose me to be his second, knowing I killed your father. He expected us to be enemies and try to kill each other."

"That was his plan all along—for me to kill you. He wanted me to find Iris for him so they could reunite as lovers. Then he'd kill me, blaming my death on you."

"It seems that way," I growl.

"So we kill him."

I grin. "Such a vicious creature you are."

She wraps her arms around my neck. "And you love me for it."

"I do. But if we kill Titus now, we will have the entire wrath of the Retribution Kings barreling down our backs. We will always be running."

"If we don't kill Titus, we will always be running. I'm not going back."

"No, I won't let you go back. You're stuck with me."

She grins.

"I don't need you as my wife to know that you're mine."

"It doesn't matter what a piece of paper says; you're already my husband."

I suck in a breath, loving every word that leaves her mouth.

"So, what do we do?"

I shake my head and laugh. "I have no earthly idea."

And I really don't. I don't know what to tell Lennox or Gage. I don't know what to do about Titus and the Retribution Kings. I don't know what to do about Iris. I don't know what to do about any of it.

"We love each other. And with your skills, I have no

doubt that we'll survive and be happy no matter what we do," I say, leaning in and kissing her.

"Don't worry, I'll teach you a few things to catch you up, hubby."

I growl and kiss her again, loving the sound of that. And I vow that someday, somehow I'll become her husband legally. Until then, I'll love her as a husband does, forever.

Epilogue

HAYES

LILITH and I hold hands as we sit at a fancy Italian restaurant together. My leg bounces up and down.

Lilith places her hand on my thigh, calming me with a single touch. She doesn't say anything, doesn't tell me to calm down, she's just calm.

I don't have to wait long as Iris enters the private dining room for just the three of us. My heart stutters at the sight of her. I don't love her. I never really did. At least, I didn't love her like Lennox loved her. But seeing her alive, after all this time, after believing she was alive and no one else believing me—it wrecks me.

"Hello, Hayes," she says.

"Hello, Iris."

She shakes her head. "It's Nova now." She takes a seat across from us like she's just catching up with old friends. Not like someone who has pretended to be dead for years, had a baby with someone in secret, and put us through a vicious competition that almost killed us both just to get to have this conversation again. I don't know whether to hug her or ring her neck.

I do neither. Instead, I grip Lilith's hand harder.

Lilith is completely calm and at ease, not at all bothered by us being in the same room. She's confident in our love. She knows I don't love Nova. She's also confident that we won't all kill each other.

I look Nova up and down, realizing she truly has changed. She's a ruthless killer now. She is no longer the sweet girl every one of us fell for. Her reputation is full of murdered men. The world has been cruel to her, and it seems she's found her own ways to get revenge.

"How?" I ask, unsure of where to start this conversation. *How did she survive? How did she become The Abyss? How did she become Nova? Why didn't she tell us all she was alive? Why hold the competition? Does she still love Lennox? Does she want him back? Will she tell him the truth? The others? Why did she tell Lilith her story? Why come back into our lives at all? What does she want from us?*

Nova sucks in a deep, heavy breath. "It's a long story. And I'm not willing to share all of it with you tonight."

I frown. "You and your games."

"You used to enjoy them." She flirts with me.

I growl back.

Lilith laughs. "I can see how the two of you were attracted to each other and why it didn't work out."

I raise an eyebrow at Lilith, who just laughs harder.

"Your daughter...she's truly gone?" I ask, already knowing the truth but needing to be one hundred percent sure Nova didn't fake that, too.

"Our daughter is gone," Nova says.

"Don't—you don't get to do that. She was never my daughter. You and Lennox were the ones raising her—"

"Yes, but you mourned her. She was your blood—"

"She belonged to all of us. We all loved her. Lennox, Gage, and I—we would have done anything for her."

A tear moistens Nova's eye. "Done anything but save her."

"I'm sorry we failed."

She shakes her head. "That's not what I brought you here to talk about. I'm not ready to talk about her."

It's all I want to talk about, but I won't push her. Nova has all the answers, all the truths that Lennox, Gage, and I have been searching for. Lennox married the Corsi heir for answers. I have seduced countless women for answers. And Gage stays loyal to Titus to get answers.

But Nova holds all the information.

"Then, what did you bring us here to talk about?"

"To tell you how I died."

———

Thank you for reading Hayes & Lilith's story! I hope you enjoyed it! Next up is Gage and Nova's story!

Join my PATREON to read my current works in progress and get bonus content > patreon.com/EllaMilesAuthor

JOIN ELLA'S NEWSLETTER & NEVER MISS A SALE OR NEW RELEASE → ellamiles.com/freebooks

Cruel Lies #4

Dangerous Lies #5

Endless Lies #6

RETRIBUTION GAMES SERIES:

Mistaken Hero #1

Forbidden Princess #2

Tempted Hero #3

Fatal Princess #4

Tortured Hero #5

Dangerous Princess #6

RETRIBUTION KINGS SERIES:

Lennox #1

PRETEND SERIES:

Pretend I'm Yours

Pretend We're Over

Pretend: The Complete Series

DIRTY SERIES:

Dirty Obsession

Dirty Addiction

Dirty Revenge

Dirty: The Complete Series

ALIGNED SERIES:

Aligned: Volume 1

Aligned: Volume 2

Aligned: Volume 3

Aligned: Volume 4

Aligned: The Complete Series Boxset

UNFORGIVABLE SERIES:

Heart of a Thief

Heart of a Liar

Heart of a Prick

Unforgivable: The Complete Series Boxset

MAYBE, DEFINITELY SERIES:

Maybe Yes

Maybe Never

Maybe Always

Maybe: The Complete Series

Definitely Yes

Definitely No

Definitely Forever

Definitely: The Complete Series

STANDALONES:

Finding Perfect

Savage Love

Too Much

Not Sorry

Hate Me or Love Me: An Enemies to Lovers Romance Collection

About the Author

Ella Miles writes steamy romance, including everything from dark suspense romance that will leave you on the edge of your seat to contemporary romance that will leave you laughing out loud or crying. Most importantly, she wants you to feel everything her characters feel as you read.

Ella is currently living her own happily ever after near the Rocky Mountains with her high school sweetheart husband. Her heart is also taken by her goofy five year old black lab who is scared of everything, including her own shadow.

Ella is a USA Today Bestselling Author & Top 50 Bestselling Author.

Stalk Ella at:
www.ellamiles.com
ella@ellamiles.com

www.ingramcontent.com/pod-product-compliance
Lightning Source LLC
Chambersburg PA
CBHW020802190726
48285CB00006B/2135